MAPS C

SJ BRADLEY

Best wishes,

−SJx

First published 27th September 2024 by Fly on the Wall Press
Published in the UK by
Fly on the Wall Press
56 High Lea Rd
New Mills
Derbyshire
SK22 3DP

www.flyonthewallpress.co.uk
ISBN: 9781915789303
EBook: 9781915789310
Copyright SJ Bradley © 2024

The right of SJ Bradley to be identified as the author of this work has been asserted in accordance with the Copyright, Designs and Patents Act 1988. Typesetting and cover design by Isabelle Kenyon, imagery Shutterstock.

All rights reserved. No part of this publication may be reproduced, stored in or introduced into a retrieval system, or transmitted in any form, or by any means (electronic, mechanical, photocopying, recording or otherwise) without prior written permissions of the publisher. Any person who does any unauthorised act in relation to this publication may be liable for criminal prosecution and civil claims for damages.

A CIP Catalogue record for this book is available from the British Library.

FOR FAITH

CONTENTS

BACKSTREET NURSERY, 2050	7
DANCE CLASS	23
THE GORDON TRASK	35
COMING ATTRACTIONS	47
WEAK HEART	61
THE STONECHAT	65
MEET YOURSELF COMING BACK	71
TORO	75
THE LIFE OF YOUR DREAMS	89
DISCREPANCY MATRIX	93
TOP DOG	111
GENUS	119
MAPS OF IMAGINARY TOWNS	137
I WANT YOU AROUND	143
HARMONY GROWS	151
DEAD LETTERS	167

BACKSTREET NURSERY, 2050

The letter came one morning as Paul was feeding the baby. He was still only half-dressed. Wearing most of his clothes, one unlaced shoe. "Oh no," he said. "No way."

The baby hammered her feet, made demanding noises.

Paul read the letter twice, and it said the same thing both times.

"I can't," he told the baby, because there was nobody else there to speak to. "There's just no way."

A woman from the neighbourhood, Maryam, ran a backstreet nursery four streets down.

He went, knocked on the door, and her nut-wrinkled face appeared, screwed up in the crack. She was old, about eighty. "Can you mind Hana today?" he asked.

Looked through the gap into the hallway, and through that past the open kitchen door. At the back of the kitchen, the back door was open, leading out into the garden. A number of children, he couldn't count how many, were hurling themselves down a wooden slide in Maryam's back yard. "We'll see," she said. "But I'm full, and you haven't booked."

He could hear one of the children opening and closing cupboard doors in the kitchen. Maryam didn't have child closers on anything. Children often came away from her house with black eyes, bruised fingers. But it was cheap, cheaper than the registered places, and she always had space to take extra children at short notice. "Please," he said. "I'm supposed to take a seat on the council this year, and I need to go down there and talk my way out of it."

"Take her with you, then." She started closing the door.

"It's not allowed. See here where it says: no children under nine allowed in civic buildings."

"Stupid rule." She snatched the letter, squinted at it. "Why not?"

"I don't know. Please, Maryam."

"Huh," she said. Slammed the door. On the other side, bolt and chain rattled as though telling a story. Then she opened it, the sun spiking into her eyes. "Ok. Give her here."

The civic hall was grey, broad, and didn't seem to want him there. It was double the footprint of a secondary school, only one storey high, and there was no obvious way in. He walked all the way around it. The North and West sides channelled a warm wind, the South and East a cold shade. He found no doorway the first time he walked around it, so he went around it again a second time, and found no way in that time, either.

He stood on one of the street side corners until a woman arrived, carrying a wide, flattish cardboard box. She walked to a point about halfway along the west side, held a lanyard up against the wall, and a door, which until then had lain completely flat up against the building, opened up and let her in.

On either side of the enquiry desk inside were two blank walls, each with a doorway cut out of it. These looked like the start of a maze.

Paul showed the boy behind the desk his letter. "This came today."

"Then you're early," the boy said. "You have to start on the date it says." It sounded as though he was tired of telling people this. "We have the system for a reason."

"But you see, I can't take up the council seat, although obviously it is an honour to be selected," he added quickly. "I've got a little girl, she's only thirteen months old, and I've got nobody to look after her while I'm here."

The boy gave Paul a sharp look. "Where's this daughter of yours while you're here trying to wriggle out of it?"

On the first Monday, the baby looked at herself in one of the mirrors on Maryam's scarf, then pulled one of the tassels towards her and into her mouth. "Don't let her do that," he said.

"Do what? She's fine."

"Her clean clothes are in there," he said, handing her Hana's bag: "A bottle, the carrot soup she likes—"

"She'll eat when she's hungry, like the rest of them do." Maryam bounced the baby on her hip. "You know, you should do something about the elderly. Look at me, still having to work at my age. It's not right, is it? Look at the state of this place." She pulled at part of the wall. An entire strip of wallpaper came away, like skin peeling from rotten fruit. "Why can't you make your new law be something about that?"

"New councillor, are you?" A tall, barrel-shaped man at the enquiry desk looked Paul up and down. "Where's the other one?"

A dried-up leaf of a woman almost hiding in the corner unfolded herself. "I'm here," she said. "I'm Safiya."

"Right, come on then." Without even a nod, the man led them through the right-hand door, then on down a corridor. He was faster than he looked, his voice disappearing as he told them: "When you think about the system we used to have – stupid. They didn't even know what they were voting for half the time, so what was the point?" Paul was having to jog frantically to keep up. He looked for landmarks, something to guide him back out again when they finished at four o'clock. But the walls all looked the same. Dirty white, no arrows or posters or notices, everything looking exactly the same as the corridor before it. "The new way is much better. More efficient. Everybody's happy."

Paul glanced back. Safiya was keeping up: she glared at the man's back as though it had a target on it. She was shorter than he was, and had to take twice as many steps to keep pace. "Slow down, can't you?" Paul said, but there was no response.

A greying wall narrowed to a point. The murmur of voices was growing louder. Then an abrupt left, and they came out into the sound of voices, a large office full of people.

They seemed to be in the centre of the building. Inside the room were smaller cubicles, all fenced off at chest height. Small square and L-shaped cubicles tessellated off central corridors, each with a worker or two inside. Housing, he saw. Road infrastructure. Schools. Everybody seemed to be doing something, busy, and they all knew the tall man.

"Monday, eh?" one of them said.

"Don't I know it?" The man paused, smiled, but he didn't introduce Paul or Safiya.

Paul looked back to see where Safiya was. She had paused a few metres behind, next to one of the cubicles, taking it all in with an unreadable expression on her face.

Their office, the one he and Safiya were to share for the next year, was a dark internal room. Desks, a lounge area with sofas, a bright red coffee machine. When they arrived, the two outgoing councillors were sitting with their feet up on the desk.

"Jim," said one of them. He had a handshake like a pneumatic drill.

Paul moved around, trying to get a sense of where he was in the building. "So, what are we supposed to do?" he asked.

Jim and the other councillor slid each other a knowing glance. "You'll want these." Jim tried to slide two ring bound folders across the desk, volume one, and volume two. "You'll have to read that before you do anything, and it's not supposed to leave this room."

Safiya flicked through the binders, then closed them with a slam. "First thing I'm doing is ending this stupid system," she said. "After I'm done, nobody's spending twelve months in this shithole ever again."

Hana seemed an ounce or so heavier when he picked her up that afternoon. "Did she have a good day?"

The wallpaper from earlier lay in a curled strip over the hallway floor. "Not too bad, not too much crying," Maryam said. "Here's what you could do. You could give all the old folks a certain amount of money a month, more than they have at the moment." Her eyes were beady, questing. "Then people like me wouldn't have to work. It's the least you could do."

"But then what would I do for childcare?" he said. "Besides, it's complicated. There are a lot of rules about what we can and can't do."

"Like what?"

"You're not supposed to do anything that benefits you or your own family. Plus, you can't undo anything that was brought in within the last five years—"

"You know, there never used to be all this," she said. "We'd vote them in and then they'd do more or less whatever they felt like. It didn't matter whether they'd promised to do it or not. We were stuck with them for the rest of the time." She started to close the door. "Not that it makes any difference."

"Maryam."

"What?" Her face was a sliver of suspicion in the doorway. "It's late. Getting dark. Do you want me standing out here in the street with my door open? You never know who might be hanging about."

"Why don't you put the lights on?"

"Huh," she said, and shut the door.

"We could ban primary schools from having a class pet," Paul suggested.

Safiya's knuckles, the colour of Earl Grey, were on the rule book. "Who cares? Who cares anything about whatever stupid rule we bring in? Nobody will pay any attention to it anyway." She gestured vaguely out towards the offices. "Waste of time, this. I don't even know what it's for, and here I am leaving my sister at home to come here every day. God knows what she's up to. She could be lying on the floor, dead." She started tearing at the edge of a page, and he watched with alarm as she flung paper dust and shreds of paper up in the air.

"Stop doing that," he said. "I'm sure your sister's fine."

"How would you know?" Safiya shot back. Her sister had the mental age of a four-year-old, she'd said, she'd gone to a special school, couldn't work. "She's not too clever on her feet. She'll try to get into all the top cupboards. You know, she could fall. She gets hungry and she will try to eat anything. Usually I'm there to stop her." She tore the next page out, screwed it into a ball, threw it towards the door.

"Leave stuff out for her, then," he said.

"Do you think I don't know my sister? I've been looking after her all my life. I know what she's like. If I leave stuff out for her on the worktops or in the fridge, she'll eat it in the mornings, and then in the afternoons, she'll start trying to get in the cupboards." Safiya tore out another page, then stopped with it crumpled and concertinaed under her fist. "At least let's stop messing about with little things, about planting bulbs in parks and class pets and all that rubbish. We need to try and do something proper."

Safiya and her sister, he had gleaned, lived together in an ageing house that always needed some attention. They had two or three cats. Safiya did as much of the maintenance of the house as she could. Their house was up a hill, remote enough that they rarely had visitors apart from a couple of younger cousins, and he understood that this was exactly the way Safiya liked it. She'd been married once, she'd said, but it hadn't turned out. "Sod this, anyway," she said. "In a minute, I'm going home."

It was only midday.

"You can't." Paul went around the room picking up screwed-up pieces of paper. There was dust and binding thread all over the carpet. She had made a mess of everything and he wanted to clean as much of it away as he could before the cleaners came. "It's too early."

"Six weeks we've been in this room," she said. "Not once has anybody come in to see us. They don't bother about us for the sandwich run. They don't peek their heads around the door, they don't come to check if we're ok, and nobody is going to notice if I leave." She got up, picked up her bag, and smiled at him. "You realise this is all just for show? You and me and the other councillors who were here before us? You waste your time here if you like." He had not seen the smile before. For all these weeks she'd been severe as a troubled past. "See you, then," she said. She went out.

There was nothing he could do. Paul stayed in the room, and went on turning the pages.

Previous councillors had written ideas for new laws in one of the books. In faint copperplate: "Government to issue limited licenses for the production of plastic items; each license will grant permission to produce a hundred (100) items of plastic, each no more than a third of a cubic metre, and no more." But nobody made things in plastic any more. It was an ancient material, ridiculous, superseded.

Further on, neat blocky writing, every suggestion to do with business. "No taxes for businesses employing a hundred or more people," said one. Another: "Once a business has been granted a license to provide foodstuffs for the general public, they should be exempt from food hygiene inspections for the next 10 years." There was a whole paragraph of suggestions at the bottom that said things like: "Allow businesses in each sector to self-regulate to free up Government to do other things."

He turned to the next page. "All fish caught in populated sections of rivers to be photographed and verified and catalogued and kept on a central database. The photos and names of the anglers who caught them are to be released once a year." This law had been brought in by somebody with the initials P.W, seven years ago.

The front door to Maryam's place lay open, gaping at the pavement like a large open eye. Getting there that morning had taken an hour. Hana was walking now and wanted to look at everything. A flower growing out of a crack between slabs. Pennies in the gutter. Everything was interesting and everything added five minutes. She would not be hurried. To see something and not look at it was a disaster worse than the end of the world.

In the kitchen, Maryam was making custard in polka dot beakers. Custard powder, boiled water from the kettle. The resulting liquid was thin, a sickly yellow. "Please don't give Hana one of those," he said.

"Why not? They all like it." Maryam stirred. "Don't worry, I let it cool first. I wouldn't give it to them this hot. What do you think I am?"

"Maryam, Maryam." A girl came running in.

"Hush now, Maryam talking." She turned to Paul. "Let me tell you another idea. If you are old, like me, you should get free electric and phone. Also—" She stopped suddenly, coughing, bending almost double. The coughs sounded like machinery breaking up a solid stone pavement. Her face was nearly level with her knees. "Don't worry," she croaked, "I'm fine." Her face was grey.

"You're not." Paul found a chair and helped her into it. "You shouldn't be looking after all these children, not today."

"I'm fine," Maryam insisted, but her voice was mist fading on glass.

Paul looked around the kitchen. There were things that he had chosen not to see before. A stack of old newspapers on the kitchen table. Old food packaging, empty, slimy with mould. Open tins with their lids sticking up, bits of food and spores forming an allegiance around spiky shark's teeth edges. "I'm calling the doctor," he said. "And all of these children are going home."

When the ambulance came, the paramedics put a breathing mask over Maryam's face and asked Paul whether he was her son. He told them he wasn't, then they put her in the back of the ambulance and told him they weren't allowed to tell him anything.

He sent her on her way with a clean nightgown grabbed from the bedroom, and a book of phone numbers from the side of the bed.

In the mornings, he dressed Hana and gave her the baby cereal she liked. She was getting big now and she liked to feed herself. It was not a success in conventional terms. Half went in her face and half all over the floor, a cornflake Pollock.

He stayed at home with her, waiting all day for them to come. Somebody in a uniform perhaps, or the barrel-shaped man from the first day. He felt sure they would notice that he and Safiya weren't there, and then a car would pull up outside his house, and there would be a knock at the door. Black uniform. Dark clothes. They would come and they would take him away somewhere, and nobody would ever find out where he had gone. Not Hana, who would be put into care, given to somebody else.

The thought of it made him watch the front windows all day. Every time a car passed, he went to the doors to make sure they were locked.

By the end of the second day (what time did they stop working? Five? Paul wished he could check the council rulebook, but it was still where they'd been told it had to stay, on the table in the office in the council building) there had still been nobody.

At night, in brief, high-temperature dreams, he saw places like Maryam's. Dozens of children in a peeling house. Faces dirty with muck and cream cheese. Children running, shoes off, in a place with nails sticking out of the floorboards. A bedroom with dozens of cots in one room, one nurse to twenty children. Feral boys like some of the ones who went to Maryam's, bigger than Hana. She would be frightened and he wouldn't be there to look after her. He woke swearing, grabbing the bedclothes. All this was something he had never thought of before. Where children went when there was nobody to look after them.

At five, Hana woke up. He got up, put her in the chair with her bowl and spoon, and phoned Safiya. She was always up early, she'd told him, because there was so much to do. All the cats to see to, and her sister. "Saffy," he said, "You've got to help me."

"If you're selling something," she said, "You might as well know I don't want it. We've already got phone and electric and we don't need insurance."

"It's me, Paul," he said. "From the council?"

"Oh, you." There was a pause. "How'd you get my number?" He could hear a noise, somebody running a tap. Safiya spoke away from the phone: "Careful, you're splashing. You only need a little bit." She came back to the phone. "What is it? Did they notice I'm not there?"

"I don't know. I'm not there either."

"Really?" Now she sounded interested. "For how long?"

"Two days. Three, now."

"So you finally saw sense."

"That's not it. My childminder got sick."

"Well." She was smiling: he could hear it in her voice. "Nobody to look after your little girl. So you're trapped at home."

"We can't both not be there," he said. "They're bound to notice."

"Huh." There was the rustle of fabric, and Safiya's voice sounded suddenly loud, as though she had the phone tucked somewhere very close to her face. "Then tell you what. I don't want to let you down, Paul. I'll go in today. Nine until four, I'll do. Nobody will ever know you weren't there. If they ask, I'll say you had to go out for a minute."

He had not expected it to be this easy. "What about your sister?" There was something odd about how quickly the conversation had turned around.

"She'll be fine. It's only one day." She added, "You know what, I'll take her to the library. She likes it. They'll keep an eye on her there."

"You could bring her here," he heard himself say.

"No, no," she said. "I couldn't ask you to do that. Besides, she don't like going places she's never been before." Her voice blared in his ear. "Zunni, got a surprise for you. Want to go library today?"

"Thank you," he said.

"It's nothing," she said. "Happy to help."

"You've done something about retirement, I know." Maryam on the sofa, her face stretched into a smirk. "I know you can't say, it's against the rules, but I know. You are a good man."

"Comfortable?" he said.

She waved languorously, eyes closed. She seemed too tired to speak.

Paul had brought a small box of tools with him. Screwdriver, hammer, a chisel for scraping the wallpaper away. The house wanted more than he could do to it alone, but he wanted to at least get the rotten, damp paper off the walls, and screw in any sticky-out screws or nails. He hoped Maryam wouldn't try to look after people's children again any time soon.

"Uzman, leave it," she said. "Don't do anything in the house. The house is fine, everything fine." Uzman was her youngest son.

"It's Paul," he said. "Uzman had to go."

She looked into the middle distance, murmuring on.

The mornings were bright yellow: crocuses and daffodils, the pale middle eye of daisies. Hana ran ahead to Maryam's. When they arrived, she tumbled in through the door, a gambolling tiger cub of a girl.

"Maryam," he called, "You shouldn't leave your door open."

Hana was out of the back door and onto the slide before he could stop her. "Stay there," he called.

The hallway was stripped just the way he'd left it, afterthoughts of glue and streaks of wallpaper. The house felt empty. A breeze blew through it from back to front. This wind had been blowing some time, airing out the house. "Maryam?" he called.

The radio was on, and Maryam was not in the front room. "Announced today, a major shake-up of the way mandatorily elected councillors will have to serve their terms," said the announcer. "From next month, no councillor will have to serve any more than six months, and those with caring responsibilities, such as those who have to care for a family member or young child, will be able to opt out."

He went room to room. Kitchen, hallway, the little bathroom under the stairs. The downstairs cloakroom was small and depressing. He had to crouch his way in and out. When he couldn't find Maryam in any of these rooms, he started going up the stairs in a hopeless sort of way.

"The changes were announced today by outgoing councillor, Safiya Bi Haq," the announcer went on, "and are the most significant changes to our system of Government in twenty years. Questions are already being raised about whether these changes in the law break any rules about personal benefit to existing councillors under anti-corruption mandates..."

"Damn it," he shouted.

Maryam's bedroom was empty, a museum. Dusty surfaces and old fitted wardrobes. Maryam's things, her hairbrush, and ageing lipstick, a TV remote, were gathering dust on the dressing table.

He went into all of the other upstairs rooms, the rooms that had belonged to her sons – Uzman's room, Faisal's room – and these were even more dusty than her own, although in Faisal's room the wardrobe had been pulled open and its clothes scattered all over the bed and floor, as though they had been used as dressing-up costumes. Maryam's things from the hospital were in a little case by the foot of the sofa. He phoned both of her sons, told them to come as soon as they could, and then called Safiya.

"Yes?" Safiya sounded suspicious, as though he might be calling to sell her something.

"Look," he said, "I told you not to bring in the six months thing."

There was a lot of noise in the background. Somebody was singing, the type of singing a person does when they think nobody can hear.

"Oh, it's you," she said. "Sorry about the noise. It's Zunni enjoying herself. Listen, I've done you a favour here. It's all over. You can go home."

"Do you know how much trouble you're getting us both into? You've broken I don't know how many rules. We could both be prosecuted."

The noise in the background stopped. "Zunni, put it on again." It restarted, and the singing started back up. "Well, look. You worry if you want to. I'm going to enjoy life."

"That's easy for you to say," he said.

Out in the back yard, Hana was running a race against herself, her face pink as a slap. Paul closed the front door of the house and looked out of the back door to watch her. "Saffy, my neighbour's missing. I don't know where she's gone."

"What neighbour?"

"The one who used to look after my daughter." It seemed to grow darker where he was standing, a cloud over the sun, things deepening so far he could now no longer see his shadow. When he looked out into the yard, he could no longer see Hana. She had run across towards the fence and hadn't come back.

There was a knock at the front door. A persistent heavy knock. Once, twice, again. It paused and then started up once more.

"I don't know what to tell you," Safiya said. "I don't know where she would have gone. Maybe you could go out and look for her. Hang on, I'll have to go. There's somebody at my door."

The phone slid away from his ear and Paul looked into the front hallway. The knocking started again. Whoever it was wasn't going away. He had not thought it would be so quick. He had not thought they would come so suddenly. And here, to his neighbour's house. How had they found him here?

"I know you're in there," a voice called. The knocking now rattled the whole house. "I can hear you. This will all be much easier if you just open the door and let me in."

Paul hesitated a moment, and then the handle started to turn. He stepped away from the front door. In the back yard, he could still hear the screams and yelps and babble of his daughter.

DANCE CLASS

She's got his eyes, Harriet. Jade green with shards of blue, clouding over in anger. Looking at her, I see his face – the ready scowl at one side of the mouth. On her it looks cute, between two chubby cheeks.

"Ready?" I say, lifting her ballet bag from the coat stand.

Silently she slides her hand into mine, and we go out into the warmth of the sunshine. I pull the ends of my sleeves down over the backs of my hands, and we turn down towards the village hall.

Walking around the curve, her satin pumps gather the dirt of the pavement. Her tutu, fresh from the wash, sticks out stiffly from her hips. As we walk by the fences, spider webs from the bushes attach themselves to the netting. It's not exactly a practical garment. If it were up to me, she'd be wearing trousers. But little girls should look like little girls, not lesbians doing an NVQ in bricklaying, that's what my husband says, and I've long given up arguing the point.

When we arrive at the village hall, the dance class before Harriet's are still in their lesson. I can hear their feet sliding over the floor. A mistreated piano jangles through the gap in the flaking blue doors.

"It's Harriet!" A girl in white tights and crossover cardigan comes running over to us. There's a whole knot of them, nice girls her age with their soft hair tied up in buns. "Come on, we're going to do some extra practise."

I watch them arrange themselves along the path. Harriet and her friend Amber stand at the front, at arm's length from one another. A line of four others settle themselves a couple of steps behind.

"Don't they look cute?" Amber's mum sits sideways in the driver's side of her Land Rover in the car park. "Like proper ballerinas."

I turn a little to her, smiling, keeping one eye on Harriet. Her toes point effortlessly over the paving slabs as she stretches into each step. It's wonderful that she has this grace. I don't know where she gets it from. "They really are," I say.

As they hop forward in a diamond, the younger girls from the class before spill out. Car engines start. Parents wave in the car park. "I've got to go," Amber's mum says. "You'll watch them, won't you?" Slamming the door shut, she drives away. I'm the only Mum who ever stays.

"Hello, Karen." Miss Elaine stands in the doorway, propping it open for the girls. As I pass, she glances at my collarbone. I realise, too late, that there's a gap between the neckline of my top and my scarf. Pulling my clothes back towards one another, I wince, touching a bruise. Her smile wavers. "How did you—" she begins; then stops asking in the middle of the question.

"Fell." I roll my eyes. "Down the stairs. Lucky she didn't get my clumsiness," I say, shooing Harriet in.

She lets the door swing closed, laughing. It sounds fake – too high-pitched, like there's nothing in it. "Goodness," she says.

I rush past her onto the bench. A chip in the wood finds its familiar way into my thigh, and I plant my feet squarely onto the floor, bracing them against the narrow wood. I love to stay at dance class. The old lady pianist starts rattling away at the keys. Straight away they start, their feet thumping the laminate. Their arms move as one, beating like goose-wings. Hammering the down-beat, they throw seed from imaginary baskets, pretending to be farmers' wives.

"And turn and turn and forward!" Miss Elaine claps along, shouting directions. "Flick your skirt and jump! Jump! – and left and left and jump! Jump!"

They're twirling and stamping, the concentration hard on their faces. Watching Harriet, I know she's forgotten the arguments, the noises that usually start soon after she's been put to bed. She's lost in it: the timing of the steps, the shape of her arms.

"Good," calls Miss Elaine at the end. "Now let's move onto our Barre work. Girls, find a space."

Running over to the other side of the room, they each rest a hand on the wooden barre. I rest my head against the cold brick. It's harder than I would like for a pillow, but this is all I have. Closing my eyes, I listen to the sound of the piano, the old lady hammering up and down the keys like a plumber getting knots out of a xylophone.

"Remember girls," Miss Elaine says, "to bring your money for the concert costume next week." Breathing out, I open my eyes. This is the end. Over now, for seven more days. "It costs six pounds," she says. "And the skirts will be ready in time for dress rehearsal a week on Saturday." After Harriet has taken up her bag, we will go back to the house together.

Skipping and giggling, the other girls scamper to the doors. I straighten, stretching out shoulders sore from an hour of sitting uncomfortably. Harriet hangs the long strap of her bag over her shoulder, carefully straightening the plastic over her chest. The older girls come in, settling themselves, leaving their bags on the wood around my seat. When she has the dark piping running flat, she raises grey-shot eyes at me, signalling that she is ready to go.

The street is full of houses like ours. Narrow, red-brick, with low fronts and leaking gutters. This is where we'd settled, he and I, taking it because it was cheap. I'd had a catalogue of carpet samples I'd been obsessed with during the months we waited for the contracts to exchange. Brown in the hallway, I'd wanted, and cream in the living room. It would be small but perfect, that was what I had thought, and it didn't matter that it was far away because my friends would come to visit. And they had, at first, but they soon stopped. He'd put them off with his glowering.

Coming in, I hear his voice from the sofa. "Where's my little girl?"

"Here, Daddy!" Dropping her bag at the foot of the stairs, she goes in. It's me who picks it up. Things can't be left lying around here.

"Now come and sit," he says. "Get your doll."

When I come around the corner of the doorway she's already on his knee, with the Baby Born she was given last birthday. Its blonde hair is bald over one eye, from being worked loose with stroking. Little hands curving, Harriet touches the bald patch, fondling the few strands of hair. A yellow frond of nylon bends under her palm as she glances up, checking she's doing it right.

"Well," he says, catching my eye. "Better get on with the tea." He stares hard at the clock, then back at me. "I'm going out tonight."

"It's six pounds," I hear her say as I go into the kitchen. Better coming from her than from me. I don't have money of my own. "For the skirt. It's for the concert. Miss Elaine said." Her voice fades under the sound of running water, and he gives a reply that I can't make out.

*

"One." Kneeling on the carpet, he counts the coins out into Harriet's hand. "Two. Three. Four. Five. Six." After the last, he folds her fingers closed tight over the top. "Now you hold onto that tight, and give it straight to Miss Elaine, to nobody else." He stands, and his head almost touches the ceiling. "What time does the class finish?" Staring down, he staggers slightly.

He knows what time, but I answer anyway. "Half past five."

Lurching, he puts a heavy hand on my shoulder. "Don't be late back." His face is close to mine. I can smell the beer on his breath, warm and stale, like a brewery carpet.

We go out, down towards the hall. It will be a bad night. Always is, when he starts early. The skip has gone out of Harriet's step and she hangs onto my hand limply, like she's hardly even there.

I squeeze her hand. "I can't wait to see your concert," I say, forcing cheeriness into my voice. I give the hand a wriggle, and she wobbles loosely from it, like a marionette.

"Thank you Mummy," she says. Her voice is clipped, as though reading from a card.

They're already in the car park, the other girls, waiting. A tight huddle of them, seven altogether, gathered around Amber. Her hair is up in bunches, and she's holding a big box of Lego with a red gift bow on one corner.

"Will you watch her?" Climbing back into her car, Amber's mum nods towards the girls. "It's just that I've got to go and pick up her birthday cake from the baker's. Here." She puts the money for Amber's costume into my hand, one note and one coin. I stare at it.

The hall door opens, and the other girls come out. They chat as they step down, their cheeks flushed pink from dancing. Harriet watches Amber shake the box. She stands very still, pressing her lips together. "I like dolls the best," she says quietly. "That's what I want for my birthday." She is looking at the other girls as though they are a very long way away.

"Come on in, girls." Miss Elaine pulls the door wide.

Making sounds of disappointment, they raise their heads and turn towards her. Amber goes in last of them, hugging the box to her chest. The soft edges of the bank note, much used, tickle the edges of my palm. Behind us I hear the hydraulic hiss of a bus pulling into the stop over the road. I close my hand over the money. "Come on," I say.

Miss Elaine watches us go, her left hand still propping open the doorway. As we get onto the bus, I see, through the open window on the driver's side, her mouth forming a round O. "Tell Amber's mum I'm sorry," I shout. It's her money I'm taking.

I know it looks funny, us getting onto the bus as we are – me in my jogging pants and hooded top, and Harriet in her tutu and leotard. We'd only walked the two hundred yards or so from our house. Neither of us has on a coat. The bus jolts, pulling away from the stop, and though she is too big for it really, I perch Harriet on my knee. Her thin legs carve into mine.

"We're going on a sort of holiday," I say. "To Auntie Peg's house."

Putting my arms around her bare shoulders, I rest my cheek on her hair. Slow-coming tears drip down into her parting. I'm thinking about her favourite hair slides, the one with the butterflies, and the nearly-full bottle of Matey bubble bath standing on the side of the tub. Things we'd be without now.

The seat beside us moves slightly, and I hear a man's voice. "You take these seats," he says. He has a whiskery grey beard, and speaks with the trace of a European accent. "Make yourselves comfortable."

We both look at him. Harriet doesn't move.

"Go ahead." Smiling, he points at the empty place.

Watching him carefully, she slides from my lap onto the cushion. Glancing down, I take her hand, and rest it on mine.

The fingers rest like matchsticks across my palm. "What about Daddy?" she says.

"He's not coming," I say. Her tutu crunches up against my leg. "This holiday's just for you and me. And when we get there, you can play with Hannah, and make as much noise as you want."

Looking serious, she pulls her hands down onto her lap. Darkness clouds her eyes like swirling smoke. I lean back against the bar, and pull up a corner of my sleeve. The marks on my arm, those blotches in yellow and purple and blue, are the last I will get. There will be no more bruises, no more marks on top of marks, no more sicknesses bleeding into one another under the skin. One step at a time I will go back to myself.

"We're here," I say. I press the bell.

Coming into view are the flats, the rows of old houses divided up into floors with panels of buzzers on a plate by the door. It'll do for a day or two, and Peg and Mark will keep us safe.

All along the bus, people start to stand. Leaning down, I scoop Harriet up into my arms. "Time to get off," I say.

*

My sister clears a space for us in the flat. There aren't any spare beds, but there's a bit of floor in Hannah's bedroom for Harriet, and a sofa in the living room for me. It was a tight fit before we got here. Now we're all up against each other's elbows and torsos, like battery hens in a tin shack.

The sofa is a wide, spongy thing, with dips in the cushions where the kids have been sitting. At sleep my body finds its way uncomfortably into them, my neck cricked out over the arm. I'm under a blanket they pulled from a box they'd not had room to unpack, wearing my sister's nightdress, her knickers.

In dreams, I'm surrounded by the smell of somebody else's life. With the wood hard against my skull, I'm in the village hall again, watching the girls skip across the floor. In the dream, I'm wearing Peg's husband's shirt, heavy with the scent of rolling tobacco, the smell of his sweat in the seams. It's too big for me and I watch the girls dance as I play with the fabric. They begin their usual formation, going across the floor in a line and triangle. As they dance their steps get harder, stamping the floor more sharply until it becomes a knocking. Aware of a change in the light, I look to the window and see my husband, blocking out the sun, a hammer in his hand. It is still dark when I wake.

The sound of knocking is Peg coming down the hallway. When she comes in, I'm standing, folding away the bedclothes. "No need for you to get up," she says. "I'm only up to make their sandwiches."

Pulling on yesterday's jogging bottoms, I see a mark on the thigh from the bus journey. A greasy pool, wide, like a slick of oil. "I'm going to call the refuge," I say. "We can't stay here forever."

"Stay as long as you like," she says.

The living room door opens again, and Harriet comes in. She's wearing a woollen skirt and a long-sleeved top with a sequinned fairy on the front. It belongs to her cousin and is too large over her. The neck drapes around her collarbone like a sack. "Don't you look beautiful," I say.

"Mark's going to get a few of your things after work," Peg says. "Make sure you tell him what you want."

It will only be a matter of time before he comes. He knows where we are already, probably, and will be sure of it the moment he sees Mark. I squash the bedclothes into the space under the TV cabinet. Two edges of the duvet bulge out like sunk parachutes. "Harriet's stuff is all in her drawers," I say. "There's a little weekend suitcase with wheels in the cupboard under the stairs."

"I'll give you his number. Call and tell him," she says.

"Thanks, Peg," I say. "Say thanks to your Auntie Peg," I say to Harriet.

Already Harriet's climbing onto one of the hard kitchen chairs, sitting quietly at the table. With her hands folded on the wood, she's waiting to be told what she's allowed to have. "Thank you," she says.

As she pours the cereal out into Harriet's bowl, Peg gives the box an extra shake. A plastic toy tumbles out into the hoops. It's in a clear bag but the green of it is bright even from where I stand. Harriet picks it out of her breakfast carefully. Holding it by the tips of her fingers she looks at her aunt, eyes owlishly wide.

"Shh. Put it in your pocket," Peg says, winking. "Before Hannah sees."

*

Her old school – a place with fat, child-friendly door-handles – is not somewhere we can go again. He'd look for us there. Pulling on a borrowed coat in my sister's hallway, I tell Harriet: "No school for you today. We're going on another adventure." The toy she won that morning – a plastic soldier carrying a moulded bayonet – is still in her hand. She clamps it to her palm, where it leaves a deep imprint. "I'll ring you when we get there," I call into the living room. Blue-striped and thin, the carrier bag rattles in my hand. I take Harriet's free hand, push open the door, and walk her down to the bus stop.

'Get there early', the refuge worker had said. But it's a long ride. Almost an hour through town, past the industrial estate and over the edge of the suburbs. I wriggle deep into the seat, trying to hide the mark on the side of my trousers. "Look for the underpass," I say. With my arm draped over the back of her seat, I peer out of the windscreen. "That's where we're getting off." The bus stops on a tree-lined avenue. A branch of pale-green ash pods brushes the top deck windows. I glance into the bag at the neatly-folded pile of second-hand clothes. As I look, the bus chugs into life, and pulls out onto the bypass.

Concrete-fronted apartment buildings with flat-plated doors meet around small paved squares. Drying clothes hang from their narrow balconies. The road rises, and I spot two rows of terraced housing. Red brick walls and bowed slate roofs. A line of doors, closed twice with metal grilles. Their front yards are littered with empty sweet wrappers. "Here we are," I say. "Press the button."

We get off, and go down to the street. Under the pass, a swing, hanging by a single strap, dangles over a patch of grass smaller than a car parking space. The fence surrounding it is twisted and sharp. It's a short row of houses, and number 36 has a black door. I reach through the outer grille, and press the buzzer.

"Karen?"

The hallway is light, more than I had expected, and brings with it the smell of fresh paint. The creamy-white glow reflects on the worker's wavy hair. She has a round face, and worried eyes. "I'm Helen," she says. "Mind yourselves on the walls."

Someone has been making coffee. The sharp smell comes strongly down towards the front door. "You're lucky you came when you did," Helen says. "A room came free about an hour ago. Come any later, and you might have missed it." She leans past us, and locks both doors. "Come on up."

The first step onto the hallway is wide. It leads onto a square little landing. Putting my foot there, I turn and glance back. Through the small toughened pane, the grill throws the shadow of a single vertical line over Harriet's brow-bone and jaw.

Helen's sallow cheeks soften. "I can see Tom playing on the trampoline from up here." She pushes open one of the bedroom doors at the top of the stairs. It whispers over the carpet. "Want to look?"

Clinging to the struts, Harriet pulls her way up. They're sturdy, taking her sparrow's weight all the way to the top. We find ourselves in a room smaller than the bathroom at home. A bunk bed next to the wall has its feet against the window. One of its planks partly covers the glass. "He's down there. If you look, you'll see him." Helen squeezes herself up against the light switch so we can get by.

So, this is it then, these four walls. I put the carrier bag down. The handles collapse in over the clothes. Behind the bed, old wallpaper has yellow flowers putting their stalks over the seams. "You can have the top bunk," I say. The wood rattles as Harriet scrambles up the ladder.

"I'll leave you to get settled," Helen says. "Come down when you're ready." The door pulls quietly closed behind her.

Twisting, Harriet looks out of the window. Down in the garden, a woman in a grey bomber jacket watches over a little boy bounding on the trampoline. It's not cold, but she clutches her arms tightly over her chest. The boy throws his arms over his head, his face red with exertion. Squealing, he jumps, throwing himself in every direction.

I reach into the bag. Leggings with a sparkle down the side unfold, sharp lines across the knee and thigh. "Aren't these clothes pretty?" I say. No skimping from Peg and Mark on what they buy for Hannah. It all comes from a good make. "And here's your tutu, look."

The sight of her pointed left toe catches my eye. On the pink silk around the arch of her foot is a tidemark of grime. "Go out and play in the garden, if you want," I say. "Get a bit of fresh air." She releases the corner of the bed sheet. The crinkles soften back down into the fabric. There are two nighties in the bag: one with a princess for Harriet, and one with Minnie Mouse for me. I take them out. "Go through the back kitchen door," I say. "I'll still be up here when you come back."

She climbs out and tumbles down the stairs, hitting every step on the way down like a rolling ball. I take out a set of freshly laundered jogging bottoms, and a fleece, both my size. The empty bag fizzes, static pulling it together around a small brown envelope in the bottom. In it is ten pounds. "Don't try to give me it back," says the note. "It's a gift."

The top drawer comes out lightly. Inside, a long black hair lays sharply across the white. Seeing it I imagine somebody tall – someone elegant, with polished nails. That was the last woman in this room – the person who left an hour before we arrived. I blow it aside and put the clothes in the drawer.

The kids are laughing outside. Off the trampoline now, the boy runs through long grass on fat toddler's legs. The pair of them run around the swing set, he with his arms raised up over his head. With the wind blowing her hair around her face, Harriet's face is flushed with a colour I haven't seen before. She's giggling, teeth shining in the early light. She shouts: "You can't catch me. You can't catch me."

THE GORDON TRASK

Annie used to say, "The maintenance men are coming any day now," always with a handful of crumbling plaster.

We spent months waiting for maintenance. Sitting together in the small office where she, and I, and Frances – a hard-elbowed woman who'd been running the Gordon Trask Centre twenty years – ran the music service. I was Administrator (Band One), so I did whatever needed doing, whatever they told me to do. Mostly writing numbers on ukuleles in black marker, or ringing round all of our registered string instructors, whenever anybody was off sick. It was me who let visitors in. From where I sat, I could see who was arriving, just by leaning back in my chair.

The Folk Club was run by two freshly scrubbed things just out of university, she with an accordion, he with a fiddle. Belle looked about the same weight as a grasshopper, and yet there was something about her: she might have been strong enough to lift a grand piano by one leg.

On the days when they came, I used to stand out in the corridor to listen. The long floor quivered as they stamped their feet, the lot of them together making a noise like a ship being hauled creaking from the depths.

It seemed right that they sang so much about the sea, since all around us the damp was getting worse. The downstairs practise rooms were so bad with it that we didn't let anybody using them switch on the lights.

Eventually, a man did come, just one. In council overalls, carrying a toolbox the size of a vanity case. You only had to take one look at him to know that he on his own wasn't enough to fix every problem with the building. And sure enough, when

I came back from switching the dehumidifier on in the big hall, he was taping the stair doors closed.

"Health and safety," he said.

Which would have been fair enough, except for that beyond those stairs was our big cupboard, the one where we kept all of the large instruments. "But..." I began.

"I can't allow you to put yourselves at risk," he said, "Nor anybody else. Nobody should go down there – it's too dangerous. What with the electrics and everything."

"This is a bad sign," Frances said, once he'd gone. "It starts with one corridor. Then before you know it, they're closing the whole place down. And we've got nowhere else to go." She led the way in, pulling the tape aside, so that we could wheel out the harp and the three-octave standing xylophone. "And now, I suppose, we'll have to try to find somewhere to put all this."

Annie said I should call the council, so I did, but there was nobody to talk to. Nobody could tell me who had sent the man, or who he was, or what we should do now that we couldn't use half of our rooms. I spoke to Estates, to Buildings & Maintenance, to Central Education, to Children's Services (which was no help at all – they had enough problems of their own), and six of the schools.

"Our building's falling down, and we've got nowhere to put our things," I told them, and they were all very sorry, but none of them could help.

Frances was not sure how long the groups and orchestras would last. They all practised in the large hall, but she didn't think it would last forever. "At this rate, they could close us down tomorrow." She had been at the council a long time and knew how to read which way the wind was blowing. *Put a licked finger out and it would tell you*, she would always say, but instead of a licked finger, you had to chart your course using meeting minutes and budgets.

"Rosie, go through all of the registers," Annie commanded. "Work out how many children use this centre every week. Draw a graph, if you have to." Paradiddling her pen on the desk: "How many are on free school meals, how many come from disadvantaged parts of the city... by postcode? And then..." she thought a bit more. "No. That will probably do it for now."

"Good," Frances said. "I can get on board with this," and she had me buy thirty toy accordions with six hundred pounds of money she'd kept hidden from the council.

When I did the numbers, I found out it was two thousand, with fifty in the folk group alone. Fifty children from the ages of six to seventeen, and half of those playing the toy accordions Frances had bought. Listening to them play, I could swear every single one of them was playing their own song. It was like walking through a Halls of Residence, and hearing a different playlist coming from every open doorway.

Annie did something with the figures, sent them to some person, though I'm not sure who. "You have to show that the building's being used," she said. "Otherwise, they wouldn't know."

It was winter by then, and we were all sitting at our desks in our coats. I had an oil heater under my desk and four in the large hall, for all the good they did. You might as well have tried to warm the Houses of Parliament with a match.

It was a Friday, a dark morning with cold creeping along every metal surface, and the stars still visible in the sky, when I came to the Gordon Trask centre, and found that I couldn't get in.

A man with a black moustache was standing in front of the doors. "No entry, I'm afraid. Building's condemned, due to the unsafe electrics. You work here?"

Even Annie wasn't there yet. That was how early it was.

"Yes," I said.

Well then, here's the good news." He consulted his clipboard. "You've got till midday to get your stuff out."

He was wearing one of those council fleeces, the ones that look like cheap versions of the ones from North Face, with the emblem on the front. *Stuff*, he'd said, as though it was only a couple of boxes.

I stared at him. Chairs, desks, all of the stacking seats in the big hall, hundreds of them. Computers, printers, the big dehumidifier... the rope lights and bubble tubes installed by a specialist company in the music therapy room at the end of the corridor. Cellos, double basses, pianos – we had six of those. Things kept occurring to me as I stood out there in the dark. I asked: "Is this a joke?"

"Look love, I'm just telling you what I've been told. You'll have to take any issues up with Buildings & Maintenance."

Frances arrived, blue-handed, muttering. "I *knew* it," she said. Face sharp as a cornered stoat. "I *knew* there was something about that fella that came..."

Annie was right behind her, wrapped up in a fake-fur hat that came down over her brows. "No use fussing about it now, Frances. We'll have to do what the man says, and get everything out."

The men watched us do it. They told us they were not allowed to help.

Teachers kept turning up, like always. Lana Handler rolled up at nine-twenty, expecting to teach a lesson, and instead got sent away with as many instruments as she could fit into her car – thirty quarter-size student violins. Peter Pelks came at quarter to ten, and he got all of the Latin percussion, including two chromatic marimbas.

Annie left at twelve to go to a meeting, and Frances at one to try and find out what was going on. By four, I was on my own with the homeless office furniture, waiting for the van to come from Estates.

Night was falling again, a velvety, indigo darkness that softened the sky like evening over a beach. Ten minutes later, a silent boy with ginger hair rolled up, carrying a euphonium in a soft case, a snail under its shell. There I was behind the clear desk, in front of an empty building with locked doors and the lights out, a receptionist for a ghost town.

"There's no swing band tonight. Didn't anybody tell you?"

The boy put his instrument down on the wide end and stared into the corridor. His eyes were the colour of puddles on a passenger deck.

"You might as well go home." I pulled the office mobile out of my pocket. "You want me to call your mother?"

"No," he said. "It's alright." He shouldered his instrument and walked away, his steps rolling side to side.

The council moved us into a city centre block, the same building as Business Services. We were on the third floor, on the side nearest the canal. My desk looked out over a tangle of wet shopping trolleys.

It didn't have practise rooms, so we had to find all of the groups and orchestras somewhere new to work. It was not easy. Not many places had enough space, and certainly nowhere to store things. The jazz band went to a church hall off the ring road, and the swing band to a sports hall in one of the schools. Those first few weeks after the sudden closure of the Gordon Trask were extremely trying. In our rush to clear out, we'd sent most of the equipment to the wrong places. Nobody knew where anything was, and my phone rang constantly. I was always looking for double basses (difficult things to lose, you'd think, but you'd be wrong), or sheet music, or somebody's set of special weighted drum sticks.

Belle called about a box of washboards. I'd put the folk club all the way down in the South of the city, because the only place large enough for them now they'd grown to the size of a Symphony Orchestra, was Wixton Academy – a specialist sports school which had a basketball court where most other schools had classrooms.

"They were in the middle cupboard, I think – in the lower corridor," she said. She was trying to be helpful: she didn't know this piece of information didn't make any difference. "With a box of whisks – don't ask – and fifty sets of stick bells... which we need for the traditional English songs. I don't know where any of them are."

Nor did I. "Let me find out for you." People were looking for all sorts of little bits of equipment, all over the city, and in their desperation, they'd picked up things that didn't belong to them. Teachers were making do with claves instead of drum sticks, and half-size student Spanish guitars instead of ukuleles. Everybody had scrambled to find a bit of space to work in the schools, a bit of corridor or a Portakabin nobody else wanted to use, and things were being left in corridors and in cupboards; getting broken or going missing. I didn't like to say this to Belle, because she had such a good spirit about her.

"Whisks," I wrote. "Washboards. Stick bells. Anything else?"

"No, that's it." She added, "I won't be able to drop the tapes off to you anymore." She'd been collecting folk songs in community centres, and bringing them to me to transcribe. Getting them to my desk now would mean catching two buses and she, like George, only got paid for two hours a week.

"Never mind," I said. "You can drop by in the school holidays, maybe."

"Maybe," she said, and we both knew she wouldn't.

It was much busier in our new office. Alex, who ran Extended Opportunities, had the desk opposite mine. He'd called the folk group CD 'dirge music', so Frances and I didn't dare listen to it when he was in. His complaints to human resources were the stuff of legend. It was frequently said that Alex was the reason why nobody was allowed to bring any type of biscuits to any meeting, ever.

We didn't want him saying anything about us, so we only ever put it on when he was out. On Tuesdays he conducted a Madrigal Group at St Thomas of Aquinas, so that was when we listened to it. Low as we could, heads together, so it wouldn't bother anybody else.

Belle's voice, clear as a brook, longing as a land-locked Fisherman's wife. George fiddling counter in the warm alto register. And the children, on their toy accordions, making the sound of a stuck and jarring engine. I could almost see the look of concentration on their faces.

We listened to it most weeks until February half-term; I had it on whilst I collated registers from the woodwind tutors, making adjustments for illness, and the shortness of that first half-term. Frances was out, looking for some of the music sets, so I was by myself at the desk.

It was distracting, to hear those sounds, and it took me back into the Gordon Trask again. Hearing George's sweet lament on the catgut, I could almost feel the draught coming up the corridor. Almost smell the burnt edges of cheese toasties from the cafe, breezing up on that damp air. I closed my eyes for a moment and felt the three of us in the small office: Annie, Frances, and me, coats on, heaters under the desk, waiting hopefully for maintenance to arrive. Before any of this had happened.

"Hey."

I opened my eyes and saw Mark waving at me from his desk in the far corner.

"Have you got an expenses spreadsheet you could email me?"

"Sure," I said, turning the CD off.

Sounds dripped in to fill the silence. The ping of the lift through the closed double doors; the click of Mark at his computer, looking through his email. Sirens from the street below, three floors down, through the windows. Somebody moving their seat around on the floor above.

Looking for those washboards was like trying to find a blunt point in a safety pin factory. There were a hundred schools in the district, and sixty music instructors on our books. Nobody ever answered their phones and if they did, they still didn't have time to hunt around. Those washboards and whisks could have been anywhere.

The receptionist at Berrybrown Primary, where I was sure they were, was a sharp woman with no telephone manner to speak of. "I've got no time to go rooting through cupboards to find – what was it again – wooden spoons?"

"Never mind," I said. "I'll come down and have a look for them myself. On Thursday, maybe."

"Suit yourself," she said, and she put the phone down without even saying goodbye.

I found fifteen stick bells sieving through the Berrybrown Primary music trolley, my writing on the stems.

"There should be thirty more sets," I said. "Where have they gone?"

"You know how it is in schools," she said. "Things get missing, they get broken." She looked at the whisks and bells

I'd gathered together and added sharply, "And anyway, you can't take those. Those are *ours*."

I pointed out my writing on the handles and she said, "Yes, I can see that, but they're ours all the same. Annie lent us twenty sets of bells to use in our music lessons."

"All right."

They weren't theirs, they were Belle's. I knew it, and so did she. But we often lent things to the schools, so what was the difference?

It was coming up to the end of the financial year, and I knew there was a bit of money left over in the budget. Frances was always trying to think of ways to use it up. This would be perfect, I thought. "Keep them," I said, pushing my way out of the door.

Only after Easter did I have time to go to Wixton Academy, on a Tuesday. There were no new bells to distribute – Frances had used the leftover money buying wheeled boxes, so everybody could move their stuff around. I had a few things I'd found in cupboards, things I hoped they might be able to use.

The place was huge, echoing – the size of an ancient theatre, and packed fuller than an inter-school grudge match. Belle and George were nowhere to be seen, and all I saw were small, bobbing heads – black and brown and blonde; children tapping their feet, keeping time. The sound of it clattered around the walls like ropes whipping a mast.

My hands were full of the boxes I had managed to fill. Odd things. I'd put in whatever I could find. Curved jingle bells and the few whisks I'd found, spoons, even. Something made me think Belle could turn her hand to these, teach the children to use them.

And here they were. Tapping, and at some invisible signal, the sound of the accordions started up. All one note, fifty thin sounds coming together to form a mourning drone: it no longer sounded like cogs competing in a machine, but like one band pulling together.

Then George's fiddle started up, and all of a sudden I heard it. Belle's voice, more beautiful than it had ever been. It was the sound of twinkling lights, drawing you in to shore; the sound of civilization after a hundred nights lost at sea.

"Sing ho for a brave and gallant ship, a fair and fav'ring breeze," she sang. "With a bully crew and a captain too, to carry me over the seas."

They were behind her, their voices, a hundred of them sounding like a thousand. "To carry me over the sea, me boys, to my own true love far away," they rumbled, voices cormorant-graceful: "For I'm taking a trip on a government ship, ten thousand miles away."

With the sound of it, I was there again, in the centre. Not in my desk in the office but out in the corridor, with the mist coming up from the downstairs rooms. I was turning the dehumidifier on in the large hall, and sweeping up crumbs from the cafe; I was setting out chairs for the choirs, locking the windows at night.

"Then blow, me winds, and blow, and a-roving we will go," they sang. "I'll stay no more on England's shore, to hear sweet music play."

All of this music in one place – the folk clubs and the Swing Band, and the choir that came in from the day centre on a Wednesday. All of it together and nothing lost, and equipment staying where you had left it. That was where I was, weeping suddenly for its loss.

"For I'm on the road to my own true love, ten thousand miles away."

Annie said, though I never saw it myself, that parents still sometimes turned up at the Gordon Trask. Razed now to the ground, with diggers fenced in by wire. They'd lose concentration for a moment and find themselves faced with a construction worker sitting on his toolbox, eating a sandwich.

"They sometimes forget it's closed," she'd say. "It all happened so suddenly."

In quiet moments, I'd rest my face up against the window, and think about the folk club practising at Wixton. Swimmers in the pool hearing the sound of stamping feet, ghostly ukuleles chiming with tales of love lost at sea, as they swam lengths in the bright, chlorinated water. Would they enjoy it, I'd wonder? The long phrases of sadness, mingling with the pop music they piped in over the diving board?

And I'd feel the slight wobble of the window as my face warmed against it, and hear faintly in the background, always, the roar of engines and the constant, driving thrum of forward moving traffic.

COMING ATTRACTIONS

Working on the Cineworld ticket counter on Kirkgate Retail Park was never going to be a long-term thing. One time, I happened to mention to a woman buying tickets for Thelma and Louise that I wouldn't be there forever, because really I was an actor, and she went: "With that face?"

Here's the thing about Wakefield. There are two things you need to learn if you live there all the time. One, people don't like it if you get above yourself. And two, the only thing you have to do to be above yourself is to say that one day, you might want to leave.

Every day, I sat behind a lozenge of toughened glass and sold tickets for whatever was on. *Armageddon, Con Air*, both of which I had seen for free twenty or twenty-five times. When the wind was blowing the right way, it got into the sleeves of my short-sleeve black and white striped shirt, and brought with it the scent of freshly-baked bread from the Speedibake factory on the other side of the river Calder.

My boyfriend, Alan, worked the box office too. At Christmas, there were six of us in the ticket office, and the queue was out of the door. People kept on propping the outside door open for the next group behind them, and there we all were in our thin shirts, freezing our tits off.

Star Wars: Revenge of the Sith had just come out, and everybody wanted to see it apart from me, who had already seen it twice, and never wanted to see it again. It was showing every hour and sometimes on the hour and half past the hour. There were more showings of this terrible film than anybody could humanly imagine. Alan and I could not understand where all the queues of people were coming from who wanted to see it.

"They can't possibly be all from Wakefield, can they?" asked Alan. Some of them were even seeing it twice, on purpose.

This woman came up with four children, two girls and two boys. The boys kept on hitting each other, and everything about them was pale grey. Their skin was the colour of a motorway siding.

"We've booked," she said. Many of our valued customers at Cineworld were like this: speaking in a brusque telegrammese. You never quite knew whether they were there to watch a film or start a fight.

I typed in the name she gave me, and nothing came up. "Are you sure it was a booking for this cinema?" We were trained to ask this, as though there was another, better cinema down the road; as though they might have accidentally come to the wrong place, as though there was anywhere else to go. "And are you sure it was a booking for today?"

"Look, you—" and I could hear her holding back the word she wanted to say, feel the rage building up in her, as though she might grab the plexiglass and try to pull it loose to get at me – she wouldn't be the first, nor the last – "listen to me, I booked on the phone this morning. Shut *up*, Tizer." One of the children had started crying, one of the boy ones, and she gave him a flick on the ear: "or I'll give you summat to cry about. You," she jabbed a finger through the glass, "you find my booking. I can't afford to pay for tickets and not get them."

I shrugged, and she stared at me, mouth hanging open like a wet sheet on a line. "This is a disgrace, a fucking disgrace," she shouted, so everybody in the line could hear. "I want to see the manager."

"Alan," I said.

There wasn't a whole lot of space in the box office. I scrambled off my stool, and propped myself into the tiny corner between my stool and the end wall, allowing Alan to lean over into my cubicle, bend the mic towards him, and fix his eyes on the woman and her dirty, feral little kids.

"Yes, madam," he said. "What seems to be the trouble?"

At Alan's New Years' party that year, the theme was 'moustaches'. You had to wear a fake moustache, draw one on, or grow an actual moustache of your own. I drew one on with my Mum's eyeliner, put on my holiday sombrero, and went to catch the bus wearing my sister's poncho.

Going to Alan's was better than going to any of the clubs. Even Buzz, halfway down Westgate, a real bin-scraper of a place, charged £15 entry on New Year. You'd have to be off your head to pay that much to go into Buzz. You might pay £15 to leave it, maybe, but you wouldn't pay £15 to go in.

When I got off the bus at the top of Westgate, a female police officer in a stab vest was giving some bloke in a new shirt a good talking-to. He was hanging his head, and he'd got what looked like sick on his shoes. It was only ten to seven.

I took the short cut past Argos (shut), down past the big Sainsbury's (shut), and under the railway bridge and past Halford's (shut). People went by in taxis, shouting "Ándale, Ándale!" out of the windows, apart from one bright spark, who shouted: "Tequila!"

Even with the short cut, it was still quite a long walk.

When the new year came, 1998, I was going to try and do something at last. That was my resolution. Try and get an acting job, or maybe audition to get into drama school. The shape of it all wasn't quite clear to me yet.

"Hi, Craig." Alan's Mum was putting crisps in a bowl in their kitchen. "Now don't mind me, I'll make myself scarce once people start arriving."

"Mum, where's your moustache?"

Alan appeared, dressed as Tom Selleck from Magnum P.I.

"I don't need one, darling. I won't be here, I'll be upstairs."

"Don't you dare." At parties, Alan's Mum went around distributing cocktails into people's glasses straight from the blender jug, and nobody ever wanted her to leave. "Holly," he shouted. That boy was a natural at projecting his voice: he really ought to have been on the stage. "Come down, and bring your eyeliner. Mum needs a moustache. You're staying," he said, seeing her begin to protest, "and that's the end of that."

As the New Year drew in, there was lots of laughter, and things being spilled on the carpet. I watched fireworks from the back step and then again, later on, watched more fireworks from the backstep. Alan and I kissed in the moonlight and he said, "You love me, don't you?"

It was cold out there and the stars were covered by smoke from the fireworks. "Of course," I said. "Always and forever."

Tiny paper streamers on people's shoulders and in their hair. Everybody was there. All of our friends from Cineworld, plus all of Holly's friends from college. Alan's Mum made her way around the party with the blender jug. Our glasses were never empty.

A party should be a crush, but this one wasn't. At a party, you should be barely able to breathe. You should have to jostle past people to get to the bathroom, and breathe other people's air. Instead there were plenty of spaces on the sofa, people were sitting instead of dancing, the back door was open half the night so people could come and go and smoke out on the back step. People were dotted all over, on the back step, in the kitchen, the living room, and the party felt empty. Even after midnight it still felt early, as though things hadn't properly got going yet.

Plus, I knew everybody. I hadn't seen an unfamiliar face yet. "Let's go out," I said to Alan.

"What are you talking about?" he said. "I can't leave my own party."

"We'll all go," I said. "Let's go into town, go to a club."

He looked at his watch, a fancy thing I'd got him for Christmas. "It's almost two a.m."

One of Holly's mates popped open a bottle of Lambrini. She poured it, fizzy and amber, on top of our cocktails. "Happy New Year!" she shouted.

The slush inside my glass tankard – daiquiri, I think, something hot pink with thick shards of ice – started to melt, the liquid inside it separating. Something oily slid out and came to the surface, thick globs of oily cream. "I knew you wouldn't understand. You never want to do anything," I said.

A few days later, Alan and I were opening up. Alan was hoovering the foyer between the box office and concession stand, a job that needed to be done about a hundred times a day, and I was hungover and trying to make sense of the popcorn.

It was a relief when he turned the vacuum off. "What are you doing, Craig? You need to get those boxes filled up before we open."

My mouth was thick, unforgiving. It tasted like a terrible mine accident in there. We had spent the previous night in one of the bars, drinking sambuca until the early hours, and I hadn't wanted to leave. It had been Alan who had dragged me away.

In another life, I could stay as late as I wanted in bars. Free drinks, a roped-off VIP area. Starting the night when the theatre closed, at 10 p.m.

I felt something sharp in my pocket. The corner of a Polaroid.

"Are you listening to me?" he said.

In the photo, I was talking, mouth half-open, glass raised, with my arm around one of Holly's friends. She was grinning, with a cocktail umbrella clamped between her teeth.

"Alan," I said. "We need to talk."

"Now?" he said. "Please just fill the popcorn boxes, like I asked you to."

"I want to be in the movies, as in, *in* the movies. Not selling tickets so that other people can watch them."

"What does that mean? What's wrong with working at Cineworld?" He started wrapping the flex around the vacuum cleaner stem. "It can be good here, if you play your cards right." He said, "What's brought all this on?"

"You've always known this is what I wanted. I told you when we started going out."

Alan stared pointedly at the empty display boxes on the concessions stand, where there ought to have been popcorn, but wasn't. "You said you loved me. Always and forever, that's what you said. It was only two days ago. Forever is longer than two days."

I held my breath and reached for the popcorn shovel, the worst tool in the world, which nobody ever cleaned properly and which had grease and black bits of popcorn skin stuck all over it. "This is nothing to do with that," I managed.

"If you loved me," he said, "you wouldn't be talking like this."

"We could make it work. You could get a transfer."

He sighed. "I'm on the manager's fast track scheme. You know that, Craig."

"Fine." I held my breath, switched on the machine, screwed my eyes tight closed and looked away. The smell of popcorn and butter hit me in a sickening tsunami. I wanted to heave into the sink. "At least we know where we stand."

Things were always quiet in January. Nobody wants to go to the cinema in the first month of the year. They're skint and it's cold.

A single Audi TT was parked in the Burger King car park opposite. I could see it from my stool in the box office. God knows what the people in it were doing. Burger King wasn't even open.

"I don't see why you have to move away. There's a course at Wakefield College. One of Holly's friends is doing it. Theatre Studies."

Let me tell you how hard it is to ignore somebody when you've got to sit next to them all day, and there's nobody else around.

"What about Tall Dave?" he went on. "He's doing a BTEC at Thornes Park. You know Tall Dave?"

"Alan," I sighed, "*everybody* knows Tall Dave."

If you'd ever taken any course at the college, you would have met Tall Dave. He'd started almost every single course they offered, and had dropped out without finishing any of them. He hadn't even finished Media Studies, the easiest course they offered. They practically printed the certificates out for that on a till receipt.

"You're a snob, that's your problem. You think you're too good for Theatre Studies and you think you're too good for this place. I expect you think you're too good for me as well."

A pause, into which I was supposed to say, that's not what I think. That's not what I am. But I didn't want to say those things, and the pause stretched longer than a rubber band, until it became too long for me to say anything at all.

By the time the couple came in, it was already too late. They looked as though they'd been up all night, giggling and doe-eyed. The girl was so thin she could have slipped through a needle, and her husband or boyfriend, or whatever he was, looked like he couldn't believe his luck. "Two for Jean Claude Van Damme," he said.

She was shaking, her little shoulders rattling like a basket on top of a washing machine. "I'm cold," she said. "Freezing."

"Here, then." He took his sweater off, and handed it to her. He put his arm around her and asked, "How much is it, please?"

Alan said he couldn't spare me for two days for the audition. The screening rooms all needed a deep clean, he said, while it was still quiet, so I had to go down to London and back all on the same day. A six-hour round trip on the train.

On Valentine's Day, the foyer was jammed with couples, and Alan was still sulking because, he said, he'd wanted us to spend our day off together, instead of me going off to try out for drama school.

At Alan's window were six single men, mingling around in the classic formation of a large group who haven't yet decided what they want to see. "Can you read out the times again?" one of them said, bald, who must have been the leader of the lonely hearts gang. "We don't want to be hanging around too long."

Two women approached my counter. Wholesome, Nordic, full of vitamins and good cheer. They seemed like the kind of people who ran a mile before breakfast, for some reason. "Simpson," one of them said. "We've booked."

"How many fancy Sliding Doors," baldie said, "and how many fancy Van Damme?" At least half of Alan's customers, I noticed, were bearded and wearing band t-shirts.

"Here you go," I said. I tried giving the women my sour look, but it didn't work. They took the tickets, thanked me, and walked away smiling. There's no getting to people like that. "Have you looked at my transfer request yet?"

I wanted to be able to move to London ready, with a job already organised, free or cheap cinema tickets once I got there.

A hard-faced woman with spiky hair, and a manual-worker seeming bloke who looked like he'd been dragged out of the house against his will, came up to my window.

"She's t'boss," the bloke said. "Best ask her what she wants t'see."

"Isn't it wonderful," I smiled, "that your husband supports you in your choices?"

She looked nonplussed. "Don't get excited, love, it's only cause I'm the one wi' money." She jangled her purse at me, a black zip-up fake leather thing with worn corners the colour of limestone pavement. "Two for Sliding Doors. Shurrup, you. Our Emma said it were one o' best films she'd ever seen."

"Your Emma's right," I said. "It's brilliant."

"You see," she said, glancing at her husband. "This young lad knows what's what."

The lads left Alan's counter, and as the next ones approached, he slammed up his 'closed' sign. "Look, Craig—"

"I've got a customer," I said.

The customers who'd already walked up to his window had, confused, tried to move from his window to mine, where there was already a set of four Mums in their best clothes, waiting. I recognised the look. Shoulder pads, pure discount fashion from the corner of the market. These ladies had shaken their best outfits out of their dry-cleaning plastic for the first time since this time last year, and they weren't going to let a little thing like resembling a 1970s bathroom suite ruin their night.

Mums always want to pay separately, and I could tell this lot were getting ready to count up their coppers and five pence pieces to do it. "Sorry," I said, "my till isn't working. You'll have to go to the next one." I pointed to Alan. "He'll help you."

"What's in London that you can't do here?" he said. "What's so great about moving away?"

"Sorry, I'm closed," I said to the goggling customers. They were watching us as though we were the latest episode of Emmerdale Farm. "Alan, I'm sorry," I said, "but it's no use you standing in my way like you are. I wanted to be able to stay friends, but I don't know if we can."

The mums were staring, confused but thrilled. One of them was gripping the other's forearm as though they were riding The Rat at Lightwater Valley. They looked as though they wished they'd bought their popcorn before they'd come for their tickets.

"Please don't go," he said.

"You can't stop me." I got down from my stool.

"Please," he said. "We're very short-staffed."

There were three people to get past to reach the door. Alan in his seat, Becky next to him, Andy at the end. "That's it," I said. "I don't see what else I can do."

I squeezed past them all. Alan and the two others working in the ticket office. I took my coat from the staff room, and walked out of Cineworld and onto the retail park, knowing he wouldn't follow.

I arrived in London with a Gola holdall, a suitcase, and the address for a houseshare in Hackney Wick.

Outside the station the sunshine was bright, the exhaust fumes constant. It was no place to stand still. I quickly found that out when I put my bag down for a minute, and a woman coming out of the station walked right into me as though I wasn't even there.

"Excuse *me*," I cried, but she didn't turn, didn't apologise. She walked on, zipping up her bag, striding away across the road.

My new landlord had seemed happy enough to rent me a room without it ever having seen me, or him me, or vice versa. Five minutes from the overground, he'd said on the phone. I moved slightly away from the front of the station, and tried to find the address in the tight swirl of print in my A to Z. You can get anywhere in London from anywhere, he'd said, it was all easy on the Underground, so really, it didn't matter how far away the drama school was, I could still easily find my way there every day, and the room was cheap, which would mean I'd have more money for going out, wouldn't it?

I'd agreed. All I needed to do now was find the house, and meet the landlord, and once I'd done that, I'd get my keys and meet the five other people who also lived in the house.

It was also outside that station where I first got attacked. My first day as a Londoner and they'd marked me out. Two big lads, jostling me either side. The book fell out of my hands and I stood myself up, getting ready to fight. Then, just as suddenly, they were walking away. One of them tripped over my holdall: "Fuck's sake," he muttered. He kept going, righting himself, stumbling almost headlong into the barriers. As he approached, he pulled a travelcard from an inner pocket, placed it against the reader, and walked through the barrier as though nothing had happened. It was absolute magic. I'd never seen anything like it before.

"Sorry," I called.

I picked up my map, my bag, and my jacket, and went a bit further along the road.

Everything along the main road was new to me. Double red lines in the road, the scent of pimento spice and garlic, spray paint and white spirit and pineapple, with a rotten drain scent somewhere around the edges. There were people in this street who looked as though they'd stepped out of the pages of a magazine. In the few minutes between me coming out of the station and walking a hundred yards or so down the road to the railway bridge, I saw dozens of people, all of them new. I didn't know any of them, and they all seemed to be on their way somewhere. Everybody carried something. A bag with the distinctive clink and drip of aerosol cans. A wooden frame, large and awkward, the size of an adult deckchair, and which they had to hold with both hands. Or else they had on tool belts, overalls covered with paint, and paint that was also splashed on their glasses. I spent quite a while watching them all, until I realised that I hadn't looked at the map at all in almost twenty minutes, and I was going to be late.

A boy went past with powder paint every colour of the disco in his clothes and arms and hair. He walked into a building set back from the road, a building which I had first taken for a disused factory. It had tall windows, large open doors, with sheets hanging over or out of some of the windows. The third and fourth outside storeys were covered in a design, and I wasn't sure how anybody had got high enough up the building to do it. Bold zig-zag stripes, yellow and grey, traversed the outside concrete in sharp lightning. I was pretty sure the council hadn't painted it that way.

He went in, and not long after, somebody else came out. I told myself I would watch for ten minutes more, no longer.

People went in and people came out of the building. The upstairs windows were all activity. Everywhere you looked somebody was doing something. There was the sound of hammering and drills. People in there were making things, but not working on a line, the same way they did back in Wakefield, at the Speedibake factory. There would be no shift change or clocking on for this lot. They came and went as they pleased.

I stayed there for quite a bit, watching. Seeing them arrive with bags or frames or large bits of cardboard and things in bin bags. Leaving with paint or clay or maybe glue on their hands and arms. I was there for ages but nobody said anything. Maybe they were used to people standing outside looking in. I stayed there with my suitcase at my feet, the holdall beside me on the pavement, until it started to get dark and it turned too cold to wait there any longer, and once the lights went on in the factory, I picked up my things, my bag and my case, and turned away to walk down the road and try and find the place where I was supposed to live.

WEAK HEART

When I was a little girl, I had a weak heart. A doctor discovered a murmur back when I was a fat-legged baby. I hardly noticed, in those days, that mother and I were alone. She said he told her to keep me from strain – any type.

Things I was not allowed to do included: running, sledging, cycling, going on rollercoasters, swimming, or skating (ice or roller). Aged six, I led the life of a Benedictine monk.

Aged seven, I became very interested in animals. Barnyard things, like pigs and cows. I thought I might become a country vet, and begged my mother to take me to the urban farm. She said: "I'm sorry, my pet. I just think it's too dangerous." She was frightened that an animal might jump out of its house and give me a shock.

Instead, we went to the library. Three times a week after school and first thing in the morning Saturdays. There were no dangers there. I used to read under a map of the world, books piled up around me like hard-backed tower blocks.

Much of the library stock was donated by the hospital. They had a lot of books on Biology and Anatomy, all full of pictures and diagrams. A boy drawn with his chest open, revealing the heart inside. Closer, a picture of the heart itself, all four chambers. Red raw and bloody, like fat slabs of meat.

A blood clot can occur in any otherwise healthy body, read one section. That part had photos. Blood clots were black, all of them. The largest had been laid on a white top and placed next to a fifty pence piece to illustrate its size.

It was a good job my mother did not know I read these books. The pictures would have horrified her. *Infection! Cholesterol! Tumours!* They were better than any horror movie, and best of all, completely factual. Malignant tumours getting fat on healthy cells. Immune disorders that make white blood cells attack one another. It is not the world that is full of terror, I discovered, but one's own body. *If the weak heart doesn't kill you*, I started to say to myself, *any one of these dozens of other completely unexpected disorders could!*

And then one Saturday my mother said, "No library today."

Breath caught in my throat. I had been looking forward to reading the final part of Secondary Conditions of the Pulmonary System. Had she discovered, I wondered, what horror stories I read every day? "Why not?" I asked.

Crouching down, she said: "I've made a very special friend, darling. A friend called Terry. He's coming to visit today, and I want you to be good." Good! I was always good. "You'll like him," she said.

I did not like him. Special Uncle Terry was broad, with a half-bald ginger thatch, and had two boys who didn't live with him. When he arrived, he put a pound coin in my palm and said, "You can occupy yourself for the afternoon, can't you?"

I said, "I'll read." I went upstairs, and he and my mother went to her room.

I was cross about missing out on going to the library. I'd finished reading all of the books I'd checked out, and so I sat with my soft toys about me, playing that each was a real animal, near birth or seriously cancerous, and each in need of my help. "Emergency biopsy!" I shouted at a glass-eyed bear. "You're too young for the glue factory!" On the adjoining wall, I could hear the sound of furniture moving.

It was too bad that Uncle Terry kept coming to visit. My mother coloured her hair dark, because he liked it that way, and started wearing a pair of gold hoop earrings which he'd bought for her. He brought me an old watch with a cracked strap, and said it was for measuring my heartbeat.

Yet he didn't come every night. Mother said he was 'researching business opportunities' on the nights he wasn't with us. She used to get skittish. Reading under the duvet, I'd hear her pick up the phone, dial, and listen, and silently replace the receiver. I counted eight, nine, ten times a night, some nights.

She was so preoccupied, she hardly noticed what I was doing. The freedom was marvellous. I ran. I jumped. I climbed trees. Nobody told me to be careful.

It was on one of these play-outs that I saw Uncle Terry. I was in the park, high up the weeping willow, when he walked by with two apple-cheeked boys who looked very like him, and a woman in impractical high heels. All of them were laughing.

They followed the path around the duck pond, and I caterpillared along the branch to try and keep them in sight. But not having had the practise at holding on, I fell. My friends later said they could almost see stars circling my head as I landed.

My mother was there, in the hospital, when I woke. Clutching my hand, she wailed: "I should have been taking proper care of you." Her hair was turning mousey where she'd let the roots grow out.

The ward was full of little girls with serious conditions. Over the floor from me was a girl hooked to a drip, her skin paler than ice. "Where's Uncle Terry?" I asked.

"He isn't coming," she said. "I couldn't get hold of him." Her voice sounded hollow, like a drainpipe.

The doctor came, with his long fingers and his cold stethoscope. "Tough little thing, aren't you?" he said. He listened to my heart. "That's a good heartbeat," he said. "It nearly made me go deaf in one ear."

"But her heart ..." began my mother.

"Yes, her heart," he said. "A little irregular. But I wouldn't worry about that." He stood up, and his lab coat fell straight around his knees. "I shouldn't think it would bother her too much." He patted my hand smartly, and walked away.

She stared after him. Her eyes were like overflowing sinks. "This would never have happened if I'd been watching you," she said.

My cast was white, fresh, ready to be written on. I wriggled my toes, knowing that if I was a horse, they would have shot me. No farmer wants a shire with a weak leg. "Don't worry, mum," I said. "It'll be fine. It'll heal just as strong as before."

"Don't worry about that," she said, and her hand closed over mine, with the strength of a blood pressure monitor. "I'm never taking my eyes off you again."

THE STONECHAT

Tan came out into the entrance, blinking. Stood, white robes flowing, on the brickwork inside the park entrance, not knowing which way to turn.

A wooden signpost by the artificial lake pointed four ways: *Haunted Valley*, said one pointer, *This way to the gardens*, said another, and another, *Nemesis*. The final arrow, blank, pointed directly over the lake, to the black castle on the other side, its stained windows, its towers, its spires. From across the valley came thousands of screams. He thought for a moment of Father Ichabod, of the life he'd left behind.

"Hello, Sir." A man stood behind a rack of four-foot teddy bears. The sound of his voice took Tan to another day. A shopping centre, a man in white trousers and shirt. For a moment, he wondered whether this man also wanted to share with him the secret of True Happiness. "Two pounds a go, sir. It's a game of skill, not chance. If you can throw, you can win."

Tan made the gesture of feeling in his robes for a pocket, but of course there wasn't one. He hadn't had money for years. Out here everything had a cost. They'd been warned about that. "I'm sorry, I don't seem to..."

He wasn't sure, but he thought two pounds might be a lot of money. Enough to buy a burger or a pair of jeans or a car. He'd once had money, known the value of things. He used to find coins in drainpipes and in the rejected coin slot of machines in car parks. Then he'd joined the Fellowship, and Father Ichabod had taught them that no Follower could know true joy if he had money. All Tan knew was sore feet and exhaustion and being dirty, and he'd wanted joy, wanted it badly, so he'd given the Fellowship all his money, moved into the dorm, started going to every single meeting, and waited to start feeling happy.

"It's on me," said the man. He held out the ball.

Three basketball hoops at the back of the stand each dropped into a funnel. "Get the hoop in the ring, and this happens." The man threw a ball into one of the hoops. It fell through, rolled along, and a bell rang. "Hear the bell, and you've won a bear. You could give it to your girlfriend."

Tan glanced around, at the signpost, at the blank arrow pointing over the artificial lake, and hesitated. There was a sound, *chat-chat, chat-chat*, like two stones being knocked together. Ought he to tell the man he didn't have a girlfriend? Or did it not matter? That morning, he'd walked out of the Fellowship and now he was here, by the mouth of the park, a free man who no longer knew what was normal. "What's that noise?" he said.

"Oh, that." The stranger reached below the stand, and showed him a tiny bird. A flutter of tiny brown wings, a feathery blush of warm pink. "It's a stonechat."

The bird made a noise like no other creature Tan had ever heard. The *clack-clack, clack-clack* of its call was a noise like pebbles clicking together in a dry valley. *Pee-wit, pee-wit*, it sang. It was tethered to a stick by a glinting brass chain. "If you really don't want a bear, you can have one of these instead."

"Any hoop?" said Tan.

"Any hoop," the man agreed.

Tan threw, but his arms were too strong, and the ball flew over the back of the stand.

"Whoah," said the man. "Never seen anybody do that before."

In the Fellowship, Tan had been a Provider. Six days a week pulling a simple mechanical plough across the fields. At other times of year, cutting corn by hand with a scythe, until his hands blistered. *Clack-clack, clack-clack*, chattered the bird.

Tan threw again. His second go hit the back of the stand, made everything rattle. Hoops clattered against the boards, and the bears jumped up and back as though they were in a disco.

"Look Mummy, a bird." A little girl had stopped by the stand, her fingers sparkly with candyfloss.

"That's right," said her Mum, without looking, "now let's find your Daddy." She pulled the little girl away.

"Last throw," said the man.

The bird's chest was pink as an azalea. No need for a key, Tan realised. The chain was thin enough for him to break it with his bare hands.

He looked at the hoop, focused on the distance, concentrated. There had been no sports in the Fellowship. Only silent reflection, and working in the fields. They had to be receptive, in case Father Ichabod should want to speak. Always had to be ready. *Chat-chat, chat-chat*, went the bird. Tan stared at the hoop, mentally measuring the distance, and threw.

Bounce, the ball hit one side of the hoop then, bounce, the other. Danced back and forth like a sparrow, then went in. It rolled down the funnel, through grey streaks left by the rain, then landed in the trough, and the bell rang. *Ding ding.*

"Do you want a white bear, or a brown one?"

Tan didn't answer, just reached silently for the bird.

The bird and the stick together were almost weightless, light like kiln-dried kindling. "Thank you," he said. *Pee-wit, pee-wit*, said the bird.

*

A white five-bar gate marked the entrance to the gardens. Lush curtains of leaves. The rollercoaster screams faded behind the swish of the grass, the thick flutter of life.

This was a green place, all the shades of it. Dark, dungeon-green leaves rose and fell in a turning sea, revealing paler green beneath. Leaves in every shape. Almost oval. Spike-shaped, six-pointed. The sweet green of the grass. Tan walked on until he found a hillock of luminous moss and dark earth and sat down. *Chat-chat, chat-chat*, said the bird. It was terrified, eyes wide. It was trying to escape, its wings a hail of bullets against his hand. *Pee-wit, pee-wit.*

"Wait, little bird." Tan gently curved one hand around it, and closed its wings against its sides. With the other, he pulled the stick, but the chain was tougher than it looked. Showing itself to be strong as a rosemary switch. Tan's scars were scented: everywhere he went, he carried the smell of True Joy.

He reached down to the bird's ankle, holding the other end of the chain, and tried again, but it would not break. "I need tools," he said. He looked around.

There was a square grey stone on a nearby hillock. It looked like a gatepost top. He carefully put the bird on it, and the chain, and reached to pick up a stone. Holding the bird under his hand, he cracked at the chain with the rock. *Crack*, went the rock on stone. The bird moved, bringing the chain out of reach, and Tan missed altogether, leaving a white mark on the gatepost. *Chat-chat,* said the bird.

"This time." Tan held the bird down, and raised the rock above his shoulder. Brought it down with all his strength and heard a *crack* like flint. "Ouch!" His index finger was scratched and bleeding. "Ichabod damn it," he said. Pulled the rock away: a necklace of blood ran the length of his finger.

Tat-tat, tat-tat, said the bird, *Pee-wit, pee-wit*. Moving now, but slowly. Tan lifted his hand, and the bird tried its wings. They fluttered like autumn leaves in a squall. The chain trailed behind it. The stick stayed where it was. The bird was free.

"Go," he said. "Go on, silly bird, go."

The stonechat hopped to the edge of the gatepost, singing its strange clacking song into the bushes. *Clack-clack, clack-clack*, but there was something wrong. It held one claw askew, as though not wishing to stand on it.

He ought to have taken it further away, Tan realised. Tomorrow the parks team might come with their nets and their chains and catch it again.

But as he reached for it, the bird hopped off the stone and fell, landing sprawled on one wing. *Chat-chat, chat-chat,* it said. *Pee-wit, pee-wit*. Tan was filled with a feeling of dread, as though his body were filled with swishing seawater. He ought to have taken the bird out of the park altogether. Further away. Somewhere into the surrounding fields. Set it free on a farmer's land.

Once more he reached for the bird, and once more the bird fluttered away, an escaping thought just out of reach. As Tan bent over towards it, reaching out, the stonechat got away. Made for the undergrowth with a hard flutter of its wood-brown wings, and vanished chattering into the trees.

MEET YOURSELF COMING BACK

Hanna was walking her dog in the field when she saw herself. The other her was coming back towards her, holding a worn red lead, at the end of which was a soft, brown, dusty dog, exactly the same as the dog Hanna had.

This Other Self came through the long grass, which swished like the ocean. She looked five years younger, as though she had just come back from holiday. "Oh, there you are," said Other Self. "I wondered when you would appear."

"What is this?" said Hanna. It was Monday lunchtime, and she had to be back at work in half an hour. She had come out of the back of the garden and up the little track towards the field. She had planned to throw a stick for the dog twice and then take him back indoors and go back to work. "I must be seeing things."

"Not really," said Other Self. "I'm you, and you can ask me – yourself, that is – anything."

Only one problem pressed on Hanna's mind. She had thought of little else for a year. "What should I do about my son?" she asked. "Almost thirty, and he won't leave home."

"Ah yes," said Other Self. "I remember."

Other Self closed her eyes for a moment. Hanna said to herself, I must be having some sort of episode, that I think I'm talking to myself in a field. She let the dog off the lead, and he walked away, sniffing the grass.

"What do you think the answer is?" Other Self said, eventually.

"I don't know. Why do you think I'm asking you? If I knew the answer, I would do it."

Hanna's grown-up son was a problem. In theory, he should have been a decent adult. In practise, all he did was go to work, then come home, where he played on his games console and chatted to strange people on the internet. He had no girlfriend, no ambition, and never did anything around the house.

"It's our own fault, you know," said Other Self. "We make his life too easy."

"Well then," said Hanna. "If you say so."

She put the dog on the lead and went back to the house.

In the days after encountering herself in the field behind the house, Hanna did the following: she disabled the boiler, so that there was no hot water. Removed all of the plates from the kitchen. Took the kettle and coffee machine to her workplace. She unplugged the wireless router from the wall, took it to a nearby scrapyard, and put it into a car that was being crushed.

As the car disappeared into the crushing machine, creating a fearful symphony of grinding, she said to herself, *Problem solved!*

At first, her son used his data to chat to his internet friends but stopped when that ran out. He said she was the worst mother ever.

"I'm going out," he said.

They lived in a small village, but if he caught a bus, he might be able to get free Wi-Fi at one of the cafes in town. At least it got him out of the house.

Hanna found she liked the silence, at first. It seemed quiet, but after she had sat for a while in the house, with no Wi-Fi, no son, and no creaking pipes, she soon started to hear things, through the open door that led to the field at the back of the house.

She could hear:

Her neighbour, digging into the soil to plant herbs.

A fly buzzing at the pane, trying to get out.

Somebody riding a bicycle along the front street, their little bell ringing.

A carer arriving to help Mrs Gondall, the elderly lady who lived across the road. "Hello Kath," the carer called. "It's only me, don't get up."

The sound of a stroller being pushed along the street, with a child inside babbling a tune.

After a moment, the dog perked up its ears, and started barking. Hanna clipped him on the lead and took him up to the field.

She waited there a long time. Hanna threw a stick for the dog, and kept on throwing it, long after the dog had lost interest in the game. She was waiting to see whether she would see herself again.

Wind rustled through the grass and the overhanging trees, whispering as though it knew a secret. The dog lay down in the grass, panting.

Hanna waited until it was almost dark. She still hoped that her Other Self would appear. That she would come almost out of nowhere and surprise her, as she had before. But by the time the stars started to come out, when her Other Self still hadn't come, Hanna called the dog and went back to her quiet house.

TORO

Toro blended the colour with a fine brush. She was painting a piece of silk draped in a white sink, showing the darkening of the cloth as the liquid drew up the weave. Her still lifes brought the eye to the points where she wanted you to look. The tutors all admired her for it.

Loud cursing came from another section of the room. In the run up to the final shows, the students were starting to panic. Toro looked from her studio into Jay's.

"When this is over," she said, "I'm going to live by the sea."

Jay paused. He'd been hammering a hanging system to the wall. On the table behind him stood something unfinished. Framed in chicken wire, a new creature, long-beaked and wide-eyed, waited for layers of papier-mâché to fold closed its frail head. "A holiday," he said. "I like the sound of that." He rested the hammer in his belt loop and smiled, head cocked.

She saw herself in the mirror glued to the wall. Flecked with blue from the oils, it was there to help her clean her face when she was finishing for the day. "It won't be a rest." Her eyes slid from her own pale, oval face, to his round, freckled cheeks. "I'm planning to work. I'm throwing myself a sea-painting residency."

Putting a hand in his overall pocket, he leaned over. There was a scrap of newspaper stuck in his tufty, red hair. "Can I come?" he said. "I want to see what you come up with."

They had been working opposite one another for three years. She stopped, taking her brush off the canvas. He ducked and then stood, waving under her nose a tray of foil-wrapped chocolate biscuits. "Don't forget who kept you fed all last winter," he said, the packaging crackling in his hands.

"I'm going to see the house next week." *House for rent. Marvellous views. Two miles from nearest village*, the curled-up card in the newsagents' window had said. *Would suit anyone seeking quiet and seclusion.* It was cheap, perhaps because no buses went near it, and the nearest train station was eight miles away. "You've got rent money, haven't you?"

The landlord, a mute man with a crumpled face, drove them to it himself. With the pressure of their final shows being off, they bounced around on the back seat like children. Jay's head kept tapping against the roof of the car. "This beats moving back in with my parents," he said. "Moving in together, you and me."

Wind caught the car, tumbling Toro into the upholstery. Pulling herself up by the door handle, she craned her neck to look for the sea. Grassy hills rose and fell, showing more hills, and more grass. The car turned up a narrow lane, and as the road inclined, she saw in the distance a white wooden house. Four small square windows at the back looked into dark rooms, and the back yard was enclosed by a rickety wooden fence. They came up a narrow-track road towards it, and when the engine stopped, Toro heard its panels clattering in the wind.

Mr Gladstone stopped the car, and they got out. The sea was lapping up towards the front of the house. Under its verandah, the toes of the wooden foundations were showing where the waves had eaten away at the ground. There were no other houses in sight. "I love it," she said.

Entry was by a side door, straight into the kitchen. At the front was a living room with clamouring walls and a large bay window, whose panels chattered in the frame. Upstairs, a large room with a wide window looked out over the sea. Behind that, two bedrooms – each smaller than the college art studios – were squeezed in side by side. A sharp wind cut through every room.

Standing in front of the top window, Toro looked out over the restless ocean. It crossed itself and ran back, throwing spits of spray over the cliff. "This is perfect," she said. "We'll take it."

They moved in the following week, and Toro set her easel up in the top room. It was a clear day, and she watched the turning of the waves. The water licked emerald towards the sand, then ran back over the pebbles in flecks of shining foam. Seeping back into the deep, it left trickles of silver and grey. She picked up her pallet and began.

The weight of Jay's hammer falls ran along the boards, shaking the wood under her feet. Mr Gladstone had given them a sharp reduction in rent, in return for the labour. At midday, it stopped. "Come down and eat," he called.

They ate in the kitchen, perched on stools. Chewing her torn bread and cheese, she looked at the panel beside the fridge, pinned home at all four corners with shining nails. That morning, it had been letting in the salt of the waves. "I've been fixing things," he said.

"So I see," she said. "While I've been painting the sea."

He lifted up the empty plates. "Just making myself useful." She stood and shook crumbs from her apron. "You get back to work," he said. He went to the sink, grinning over his shoulder at her. "That's what you're here for." Going upstairs, she heard the clink of plates.

It had changed, the water, taking on a deep colour in the shadow of the cliffs. The painting she had started that morning showed colours bright, tranquil, the sea at rest. Taking the canvas from the easel, she rested it up against the wall, and started again.

She finished work at dusk and went to bed soon after.

Laying in the narrow bed, she dozed with her arms crossed across her chest. A crack in her window whistled with the sound of the waves, breaking on the back of the house. She imagined the pair of them being carried out to sea. Sleep took her with the sensation of being on a raft, rocked high by an unceasing storm.

The next day was clear. She ate her cereal leaning against the living room window. "I thought I could hear the sea last night." The sun was landing brightly on the flaking bolsters of the porch. "Coming right under the house."

"I've been thinking about that," he said. "And I came up with an idea for strengthening the verandah."

Grains of saturated cereal made soggy islands in the last of the milk. "You ought to be working on your art, Jay," she said. "Not being a handyman."

"This is my work, for now." He rested a hand on her shoulder. When he took it away, it left a warm mark, crinkling on her shirt. "You go and get on." He took the bowl and cup softly out of her grasp and went into the kitchen.

She went on painting. The long glow of autumn gave way to winter. When a cold wind bit around the outside of the house, she didn't feel it in the studio. Jay's work on the walls had sealed it out. He had put a little wood-burning stove in the top room to keep her cosy. It allowed her to put it all to canvas: the pinked cream of the foam, the navy of the depths in the quickening of the dusk; flinted gridelin as the sky clouded over.

When spring came, the look of it changed again. The ocean lightened, reflecting the cornflower blue of the sky. It came suddenly, the difference, catching her off guard.

"Look first," she said to herself one morning. "Take a really good look." Going to the window, she heard a thud as Jay's toolbox landed on the decking. He had said, with the weather warming, that he was going to start pinning the underside of the house.

The tide was further away than she had expected. From the front of the house to the rugged faces of the hills, the sand was dry. Picking up her binoculars, she trained them to the water's edge. The sea was turning back on itself. It made a smooth round shape as it crashed back to the horizon. Bobbing in the shallows, a sandpiper shook salt from its eyes as the water burst over its head.

"Jay!" Toro folded her easel. She put it under her arm and ran down the stairs. Its legs caught every step. "Jay!" He was at the front of the house, leaning over his workbench, his saw halfway through a plank. "Look how far the sea is out," she said. "The waves are turning the wrong way."

Flecks of wood-dust were flung out from the cut by the motion of his hand. It sawed steady in, steady out. "Toro, you have some very strange ideas."

"It *is*," she said. "I'm going to walk down to it. Will you keep an eye on me? In case the tide suddenly comes in."

Reaching into his pocket, he took out a handful of nails. A long, oxidised nail with a little head rested against the crook of his thumb. "I'll be here. In case the tide suddenly comes in." He shook his head. "I'll be waiting for you, like I always am."

The tubes – white, black, blue – warmed in her hand as she walked. Birds, flying overhead, cast shadows over the perfectly flat sand. Toro's were the only footprints. Walking between the high cliffs, she took off her shoes, leaving them there in the shape of the way she stood.

Trails of seaweed lay like witches' hair. They popped when Toro stepped on them, as she came close to the sea. Bubbles formed a semi-circle around her toes. They stayed where they were, the waves, turning their smooth arcs towards her. She opened up her easel and put it on the sand.

She opened one of her tubes and put paint straight onto the canvas. A fat worm of white scalloped into the shape of the waves, becoming sky when she added blue. When she looked up at it properly, she saw it bolder than the sea. The brightness of it hurt her eyes.

Bending, she put her brush into the turning waves, and the reflection of the sky broke and split. She squeezed what colour was left out of the hairs, and the water ran over her fingers. It settled in the lines in her prints, and she turned to look at the house. It stood on the edge of the bay like a tiny solitary tooth. Jay, the size of a comma, was driving nails through the porch floor.

The sound of rocks falling made her turn. At the top of the cliff stood a young man with a bicycle leaning between his legs. His curling brown hair came to an end at his wide jaw. "I know you," he called.

She pushed blue into the corners with her brush. "I don't think so," she said.

"I do. You're from the house over there. I'm Sam. I deliver your milk and your eggs. Give them to your boyfriend, normally." The day being still, she could hear his voice very clearly.

"My housemate," she said. "You give the milk and eggs to my housemate." She looked up. He was smiling all the way into the corners of his hair.

"Is that what he is?" he said. Then, pointing at the easel: "When's your first exhibition?"

"There isn't one," she said. "Not yet. But if you want to see the paintings, they're all in the house. Come any time."

"How about tonight? I'll bring a bottle."

"Why not?" she said. Then she turned and put her attention to the problem of the sky. The sea, as she had painted it, had come better than she remembered. The curve of the strokes seemed to show the waves play, their movement as they sank down into the body of water. Already the day's work was turning out well. When she turned back up to the cliff, Sam had gone.

When she was done, she took the work carefully from the easel and walked back to the house, stepping back into her shoes under the cliff.

Jay was sitting on the porch. "Thought you might be hungry," he said. There were two slices of cake on a plate, and two bottles of beer. "I saw you coming back."

"The sea is still there. It hasn't moved a bit." She jumped onto the verandah and noticed how sturdy it felt. The old rotten struts, ripped out and stacked, lay in a pile around the side of the house. "This is great," she said. "I've been worried all winter that the house will be swept away." Taking a swig of beer, she rested her forehead against the bannister.

He picked up the canvas. "This is the best one yet."

"I could see the shades much better, standing right by it." She broke off a corner of cake. The icing stuck to her fingers. "And I saw Sam, the delivery boy. He's coming over tonight."

"Coming here?" Jay looked out to the cliffs. His eyes skipped along the horizon.

"He wanted to see my pictures."

"Everybody should see them," he said, faintly.

Taking the canvas, she hopped down. "I'm going to put them all up before he comes. Can I take some of these nails?" He sat looking out as she rattled, humming, amongst the crowd of tacks next to his leg. She found a handful of similar length and slipped them into her pocket. "Can I borrow your hammer?"

He moved. "You ought to let me do it. If you hit any of your fingers, you won't be able to paint." Throwing back his head, he swallowed the last of his drink. "Come on."

In one painting, a restless ocean threw waves over the rocks. In another, three tiny white boats floated close to the cliffs. And in one still wet, the waves, a close tone to the sky, turned themselves over on their heads. "When I do an exhibition, I'll do them just like this," she said, as he hung them. "All along the wall, together, exactly like that." She was feeling a little lightheaded from the beer.

He tiled them in similar shades. Dark blue at one end, graduating to periwinkle at the other. "I hope he likes them," he said. He went out of the room.

The sea had turned. The tide made a shirring sound, coming back up the beach. Sitting on the studio floor, she heard Jay lift the decaying wood, and take it around to the back yard. Light was sliding out of the room. On the table, her things, the tubes and the board and the brushes, huddled in the darkening room like strange beasts. Shade settled into every corner. There was a knock at the door.

"Nice place," Sam said. He'd brought red. "How long are you planning to stay?"

"We've been here seven months already," she said. "And I don't have any plans to move away." She led him up to the studio. The shapes were failing in the gloom.

"Wow," he said. He put his hands in his pockets and stood in front of the wall. She studied his profile. A strong nose, sharp like the cliff; round lips, pursed, like washed-smooth pebbles. She went downstairs to get glasses and when she came back, he was sitting cross-legged on the floorboards.

The wine left a grainy black sediment around the stem-head. She sat, the moonlight landing on her forearms, her knee touching his.

"You're an artist. You should always paint," he said, voice thick with the drink. He poured the last of the bottle into her glass. A dribble of dark red, tinged with black, landed in the fat part of the bowl. "Don't let anything stop you."

"I won't," she said.

The side door slammed, and she heard Jay in the kitchen. Pans and handles banged, the tap squeaking as he turned it. The oven door handle clicked, and its metal shelves rattled. She got up. The houses of the village had their lights on, like copper tongues in the distance. The black mass of the sea caught their reflection on crests sharper than fallen pins. "I've never thought of painting it at night," she said, to herself. "In the dark." She turned for her board and, reaching for it, saw two. She closed one eye. Laughing, she said: "Sam!"

She twisted on the balls of her feet. He had fallen asleep on the floor. Pulling a blanket over him, she went to her own bed.

In the morning, the smell of strong coffee thundered against a hard feeling in her head. She got up, clutching the duvet to her, and looked around the studio doorway. Sam had gone.

She went down into the living room. "You might need to make more coffee," Jay said. He was wearing his dungarees, the ones he'd worn every day in college. "I've only got a two-person pot."

"Sam left early, anyway," she said. "I don't think he really meant to stay."

The surface of his coffee rippled. A sigh came out of him, like a breeze moving spring leaves. She went to the window. A tiny black bird was running across the dry sand. The sea, having gone back beyond the cliffs, looked no wider than a silver ribbon.

"It's doing it again. Like yesterday." The coffee tasted like sour gooseberries. She put the cup down on the sill. "You should make something with those pieces of wood," she said.

Resting his head on the chair-back, he stared vacantly out of the glass. "I feel a bit tired," he said. "I didn't sleep all that well."

"Then have some more coffee," she said. "I'm going down to it again."

"Toro, why did you bring me here?"

"You wanted to come," she said. "I thought you were going to work. It's not my fault if you ended up not doing that."

Carrying her easel under her arm, and her paints and brushes in a knapsack, Toro walked down to the edge. The retreating sea had left a line of the dead. Crabs not quick enough to move lay dried up on their pink backs on the hard rock. An anemone stuck its dried fingers up through a line of seaweed. She trod carefully among empty limpet shells.

Settling her easel in the shadows of the cliff, Toro took out her paints. A small white pleasure boat, its hull resting on jagged rocks, was lifted and knocked, lifted and knocked, by the softly-turning waves. She noticed a paleness on the surface of the water. A scuffed-looking sky of white and grey hung overhead, and out in the depths, the ocean looked still. Taking off her shoes, she put her feet in the sand. A gritty feeling worked its way between her toes.

"There you are." Sam was coming down a steeply-cut path towards her, wearing a grin like a cutlass blade. "I've been looking for you."

She had been about to start, but instead slid the tubes into her apron pocket.

"I went to your house first," he said. "To say sorry for falling asleep. Jay was building something in the back yard. It looked like—" He paused, a half-smile playing around the edges of his lips. "Well, I don't know what it looked like, actually. Either way, he didn't seem all that pleased to see me." Scraping his boots against a sharp rock, he said: "I'm having some people over tonight. Why don't you come? Have a change of scenery."

The sea and the sky, the sky and the sea. It was hard to know where to start. She turned and looked, again. Distantly, she heard the sound of hammering. It echoed between the cliffs, the sound of Jay making something from nothing.

"I don't know, Sam," she said. "I'll see." Far away, an ocean liner the size of a centipede crossed the horizon. She heard him scrambling back up the path.

Looking down, she saw the sea leaving behind it a hard black line. Between her toes were specks of glass and ash, shards of granite and wood-splinter. She stopped staring at the sea. Using a corner of her brush, she made up a picture with dots of colour, painting the ground beneath her feet. As the light crossed over to the other side of the bay, she turned to look at the house, hardly larger than a dust mote.

She crammed the stand under her arm, and carefully took hold of her day's work. As she walked towards it, the house became larger in increments tinier than a brush hair.

Standing in the short grass at the side of the house, she looked into the back yard. Jay had used the old wood to make a wooden bird. Its chest was fat and its neck narrow, and its joints bold and angular. He was nowhere to be seen.

On the kitchen worktop was an empty skeleton of bended wire. She recognised it. At the end of the summer there had been a piece left over, something he'd never finished. It was to be a new beast, one with a long elegant neck and a broad, serene face. He'd shown her the sketches. Beside it was his hold-all, gaping open and half-full with clothes.

"You've started working again," she shouted up the stairs.

"Yes. The idea came to me today." He came down, carrying an armful of trousers and pants. "You were right to say that I'm more than just a handyman."

Lightly, she touched the wires curving over the empty skull. "What's it going to be?"

"It's going to be part of a flock of birds – a whole collection. I'm going to do a wood full, and I need a lot of space to do it." He shovelled the clothes into the bag.

Her canvas fell unevenly, loudly, onto the top. "Space, what sort of space? You're going now?"

"Mr Gladstone's coming to take me to the station," he said. He moved his tool-box closer to the door with a foot. "I've wasted too much time by not working already."

"I don't want you to go," she said. "Can't you do it here?"

"It's already settled." In his embrace, she smelled emulsion and varnish, and felt the warmth of a house with solid walls. "You don't need to worry about the rent for this month. I explained everything to the landlord." Outside, a car engine chugged close. It stopped at the gate, and its door opened. "You'll be fine, Toro. You generally are." The zip whistled as he drew it closed. "I'll write." He went out, closing the door behind him.

The waves were hitting the front of the house. She went upstairs, and leaned the day's canvas against the studio wall, underneath the others. Her paint tubes echoed as they hit the floor. Kicking them aside, she fell into a sitting position under the window.

The water licked around the thin part of the verandah supports. All night she sat listening to the tide, making that *wish, wish* sound as it came up to the house. A white rhombus cast by the moon shifted across the floor. She crawled into bed only as it sank beyond the hills. She dreamed of solitary gulls and brittle half-shells, and of being alone in a heaving row-boat far from land.

In the morning, she was woken by the sun landing hotly on her eyelids. The house was silent. She got up, the crinkles in her skirt falling loose, and went to the studio window. A long expanse of sand, pale and clear, led all the way past the cliffs, further than she could see. Gone were the crab-carcasses and the long trails of seaweed. Under the hills she saw the little white boat run aground, its hull tipped up towards the cliff. There was nothing else between the house and the horizon. The waves had washed everything clean away.

THE LIFE OF YOUR DREAMS

They were giving her everything she needed to build the rocket. Bolts, sheets, fusion conversion unit, fuel pipe, sparkers. All of it in the package, sliding down the ramp towards her. Anna watched a Ganglian worker push the box away from his truck, where it landed in the barn entrance, half in shadow.

Beetles crawled around the doorway, segments of their long brown bodies glowing bronze in the sun. Anna watched the worker turn, get into his truck, and drive away without a word. That would be the last Anna saw of the Ganglians for twelve days.

She tore the lid open. A sheet was taped inside. "Anna 51628: To be returned if incomplete 96.84, and worker 51628 to return to usual duties." The glare of the sun landed hard on her shaved head. Inside the greenhouses, hydration sprays pulsed through polycarbonate sheeting. At the near end, she could make out two shapes: men standing side by side, their hands in the rhyberry branches. They were picking the green-gold fruit, and laying them into punnets. The Ganglians didn't like their berries crushed. Even a single bruised fruit meant a whole box discarded. The work quota was eight punnets a day. Work over quota, and you could earn an extra stamp on your clock card. Twenty stamps for a bottle of vodka the size of a bottle of nail polish. Forty for a sanctioned hour off work. Five hundred for a rocket.

Inside the box, lifeless dials were mounted on a board. They met a curved tube shaped like an exhaust. There was a sound in a corner of the barn, and Anna turnedG to see a man wearing goggles, working on his own kit. He had the metal sheeting welded together in a long hexagon. The pieces formed a narrow column, too thin, too close, for an adult to get inside. Wiping his brow, the man pushed his mask back. "Hello there," he called. "You here building your rocket pack?"

Anna allowed the components to fall back into the box. They landed with a soft clatter. "There aren't any instructions," she said. "I don't know where to start."

"Come down," he said kindly. "Have a look at mine."

His corduroy trousers were scorched, burned flat with sparks from the work. Between his feet stood a small engine. What looked like a thick rubber band held one cog to another. The whole mechanism together was no larger than a driver for a toy train. "Is this it?" she said.

Talk in the sleep tins said a rocket could get you home. Back to Earth, with its high waters and scorched ground. It was a place Anna had once been desperate to escape. *Live the life of your dreams on Ganglian-A*, the advertisements had promised, and Anna had believed it. She and a friend, Urtka, had scrabbled the money together to pay the passage to get here. Anna had got hers hustling pool. Urtka, staying out late in the evenings, had brought home a twenty here, a twenty there. Anna hadn't wanted to ask how she'd come by it.

The carrier they'd come in was a vessel shaped like a tumble drier drum. Anna had ridden with somebody's feet in her nose, and somebody else's child under her armpit. The air had been too stuffy to waste it talking. Feeling the metal tremble through the mass of bodies, Anna had been able to make out the top corner of Urtka's ear, squeezed next to a beard and an elbow. Coming past Mars, past Saturn, or so Anna imagined, Anna felt the sides grow cold, and tried to count the Earth days. If there was a toilet, none of them ever found it. She rounded Pluto with somebody's urine dripping down her cheek. It is close now, she told herself. It is close. She thought it worthwhile for what awaited them at the other end.

Weeks later, a corner of the ship hit solid ground. The bottom end opened, and their bodies were shaken out. As she fell, Anna saw arms and legs frozen to the sides of the can, torn loose from their owners. She landed on a pile of the dead. Scrambling free, she'd seen Ganglians in work uniforms shovelling corpses into a pit by the landing pad. It looked dug for the purpose. Anna climbed to the top, and saw Urtka's lifeless form tumbling into the hole. Work started on the second day.

The man said: "I was an engineer, back on Earth. And sometimes little things can pack a punch. They're more powerful than you'd think, to look at them." Up close, his rocket looked even more like a child's toy.

"This doesn't look big enough for a dog," she said.

He smiled sadly. "You catch on fast," he said. "Most people don't realise until they've put it together. They hope it'll seem different out of the box." There was a mark around his eyes, a red rim left by the goggles. "Twelve days off work isn't to be sniffed at, though. I come here as often as I can afford to. It's the best reward you can buy, I think." There were tools mounted on the wall beside him. A hammer and a wrench hung on hooks beside a screwdriver and a set of pliers. "Well," she said, "that's not enough for me."

Anna took an adjustable spanner from the rack. There was a gap in the barn wall, and you could see the greenhouses through it. She could see the spray from the irrigation system splashing against the insides of the plastic. The silver bolts gleamed in the heat. They lashed the sheeting to the frame and held the roof and walls steady. Anna looked down at her own hands, dry and cracked from working all day in the wet. She imagined loosening the bolts, seeing the greenhouse lid slide loose, the copper glare of the nearest star shining on the workers' skin as the walls and roof fell down.

Down in the corner of the barn, the man hammered tacks into their homes in his project.

Anna slid an adjustable torque-wrench into her pocket. "I'm going to work outside," she said.

DISCREPANCY MATRIX

There were nine of us in the office when the email came. Tunde, sitting at the hot desk opposite, made the sound of a flat tyre running into a hard shoulder.

"Not again," we said. "At this rate, there will be none of us left."

We were down to around sixteen people, social workers, and one manager. None of us had seen the manager, Linda, in about three weeks.

I shifted in my chair, a lumpy cushion of coats, cardigans, scarves. When other people left and didn't take their office cloaks, I inherited what was left. Outside the sun was still clutching the horizon as though afraid to let go. It still felt cold to me. It always felt cold to me.

Tunde was deep into a birthday cake that had been left in the staff kitchen. There was pink frosting all around his mouth. It wasn't even nine a.m. "Where'd you get that?" I asked. "I haven't even seen Halimah this morning."

"When they start the restructure of the citywide social work teams," he said, "there will be no time to be sitting around birthday cake." He added: "She went on her visit first thing. She hasn't even been into the office yet."

I went out to my patch of houses. Our part of the city was all fenced off. It was low pebble-dashed houses and little gardens. It was people standing in streets and shouting across fences. This was a noisy part of the city. Quad bikes in the day and fireworks being thrown down the streets at night. The noises were inside the houses, too. In the house I'd grown up in, there had been empty doorways where doors should have been.

Loud, echoing concrete floors, no carpets.

The rain outside was a punishment. I was knocking on a door and a dog was throwing itself against it from the other side. I'd been at the department a couple of years and I was getting a lot of experience at these things. Identifying breeds by the way they throw themselves at a locked door. This one was a Staffie cross.

Somehow, by the way, the dog threw itself at the door and the silence inside I knew this was a door that wasn't going to be opened. They were inside, statues. Shushing each other in upstairs rooms. I could cup my hands and look through the living room window, but there was no point: there would be nobody there to see.

"Mrs Wright," I called, "Mrs Wright, are you in there?"

There was a boy lived in this house, Jayden. A teacher from the school had called the duty line. There was this boy, Jayden Wright, and the school had concerns. "The boy looks as though he's seen a ghost," said the notes. This was a boy who ate six slices of toast at breakfast club, who took food from other children's plates. A teaching assistant had seen him draw an unfinished apple core from a bin. The Head gave him extra food: Pop Tarts, waffles, sandwiches, and the boy, like the Hungry Caterpillar in the story, ate all of it, and still was hungry afterwards.

A few weeks after the first call to the duty line, the school had called again. It was the Head this time. He'd asked Jayden's Mum at school pick-up time, *were they doing OK? Were they managing, did they need a referral to a Food Bank?* And the Mum had said they were 'fine', and she'd taken the boy away as normal, and then the day after that they'd said the boy was 'too ill to come to school'. They'd had him at home for almost two weeks now, and the school were worried.

All this had happened two to three weeks ago, the amount of time it had taken for the referral to get to me. I would have liked to have seen it sooner. But I was drowning, drowning, drowning, like we all were, under the weight of files, with the weight of need in the city, waking up in the night with the feeling of being crushed in a vice, sharp in the certain knowledge that I'd missed something, that it was only a matter of time before something terrible happened.

This was not a surprise visit. The Mum knew I was coming. 'Any time Tuesday,' she'd said, and here I was standing out on the doorstep, the rain turning my trousers to wet washing against my legs. "Mrs Wright," I shouted, "Mrs Wright!"

Sometimes when people hear the voice of the social worker at the door, they stop pretending they haven't heard you knocking, and they answer. I could have called through the letterbox, but I wasn't about to stick my fingers through this door, not with this dog. Linda had been very clear that none of us was expected to put ourselves in any danger.

"Ms Wright," I tried, one last time, and nobody answered. I turned away and walked back to my car.

Linda was a fan of the matrix. Not the film, the social work tool. A Discrepancy Matrix separates what we know from what we have heard. Linda likes us to use it a lot. It allows us to close a lot of cases.

Begin with the notes. What people have told us, what's come through on the duty line. In a case like this, you don't have the evidence of your own experience. All you have is what other people have told you. Everything you have is written and plotted on a graph. If the dots gather in the top right quadrant of the tool ('Known,' 'Very Likely'), that is when you absolutely must act. If everything gathers bottom left ('Very

Unlikely', 'Not Known') then all you have is speculation, pure gossip, and when the tool comes out like that, Linda is against pursuing things further. We are hundreds of cases deep in this department. We've got so many children and families we don't know how the city fits them all in. We pursue the cases where we know we can help, where what we have are solid facts.

"Anybody sitting here?"

Halimah appeared when I had the axes out and was writing dots on the paper for Jayden Wright, a child I had never even seen.

She put her wiry body in the chair opposite, where Tunde often sat. "I hate hot desking, don't you?" she said. "It sort of makes you feel like you don't belong. Or is that just me?"

"Not just you," I said.

"You'd think there would be a desk for everybody," she said, "Since there are so few permanent staff. Here, what d'you reckon to that email this morning, then, eh?"

Halimah was a low talker, an expert in making sure only one person heard the things she said. When she spoke, her words were only ever heard by the person they were meant for. That was how she got away with so much. She was an agency worker, a bank member of staff, and she moved from place to place around the district. At the moment, as she had been for a couple of months, she was with us in the north east of the city.

"I saw it." I stopped working. "Are you on our distribution list now, then?"

"No," she said. She had a laptop from one of the lockers, a thing as old as the building itself, and put it on the desk. These things weighed a ton. When you pulled them out of the lockers, they strained your shoulders. If you dropped it, it would break your foot. "Dave forwarded it."

Halimah was on half the distribution lists in the city, from having moved around so much. If you wanted to know anything, ask Halimah. She had bits of information from all over. "You know what else. Morale is so low in some places here. There was a long email thread from my old team in Harehills. I'll tell you, that is one unhappy team. I swear none of them speak to each other. Everything they say is over email. They're typing out complaints that nobody ever washes up, and that whoever is stealing the teaspoons, needs to bring them back. Who steals teaspoons? You can get them in IKEA for a quid." All social work teams gossip and their news passes through Halimah. "You know what I think?" she said. "That team is draining people like water from a dyke. They're trying to look over a part of the city with thousands of families, and there's only about six left in the team. You know what this restructure is about? If you ask me, it's centralisation. Trying to save money, and teams, by putting us all together. There's not enough people over there, so they'll get social workers from over here to make up the shortfall."

"You're joking, aren't you?" I said. "We haven't got enough hours in the day."

"Either that, or sooner or later they'll cut the whole lot of us. Everybody in social care, make us all redundant, *poof!*"

"They can't do that," I said. "Do you even know how many cases come in here every day? We can't get to them for weeks and weeks." I laid my pen across the discrepancy matrix. A diagonal line from Absolutely Certain, Not Known, to Very Unlikely, Known. "These managers, do they think we're all sitting on our arses all day reading magazines? You'll be alright," I said. "It'll be more work for you, if anything. We'll probably all be temping before the year's out."

This was the fourth time. No, fifth. It was the fifth time in six years I'd been through this. Restructures and redundancies and departments losing staff by attrition. People left and were not replaced. Their cases were shared out among remaining staff who were hanging on by their nails.

"No, no, no. No way lady, no way. You'll be fine, you and your job. You're needed. You'll be fine and a half. How long you been here?"

"Twenty years, I think," I said. "Maybe twenty-five."

"You shut up." She opened the creaking laptop with a grin. "Twenty years ago, you weren't even a thought in your father's head."

"Come on. I'm thirty-two."

"That I don't believe." Reached over the desk, poked me with a bony finger. "You're not a day over twenty-one. You couldn't even get in to see an eighteen movie. What's your secret?"

Outdoors was a cold bitch, the air so cold you could slip on it just taking it into your lungs. It was Norway in the car park, one of those days that makes you wonder whether you'll ever see the sun again.

This time they didn't know I was coming. Social workers are sneaky, that's what families always say. *They don't come to help, they come to trick you.* That was what I was doing to the Wrights. I tricked them by parking my car on another street, and hammering the door the way a delivery driver would. As though I was getting paid per parcel. As though I had twenty drops to make in an hour and couldn't afford to wait. Loud enough that they could hear it if they were out smoking on the back step.

Knocking like that almost always works. People are very likely to answer if they think you're there to bring them something, much more so than if they think you're there to take something away.

The dog barked then quieted. I heard the noise of somebody shutting the dog in the back room. Steps as they came to the front door.

Her face fell when she saw I wasn't from DPD. Mrs Wright was small, crumpled, her face an unopened envelope that nobody wants. "Who are you?" she said.

I told her I was from social services. That I'd been before, but that nobody had answered the door.

"Oh yes, that's right," she said, with a big fake smile. "I must have got the wrong day. Come on in."

The house was not too bad, clean-ish, unless you counted the dog hair. Surfaces and floors looked like they'd been wiped in the past day or two. No mould on the walls. Not much in the kitchen cupboards, though.

She showed me what they had. Half a tub of gravy powder, one tin of beans, one small tin of spaghetti hoops. "There's a bit of stuff in the freezer, too," she said. "But I won't show you that."

"The school are worried about Jayden," I said. "They say he's always hungry."

"Jayden's fine," she said. "I love that boy to my very bones. I'd never do a thing to hurt him."

"They said he arrives at school saying he hasn't eaten since the previous lunchtime."

"Boys." She clucked, rolled her eyes. "He's growing. Prone to exaggeration."

"If you don't mind my saying so, you don't seem to have a lot in."

"Haven't had time to get to the shops," she said. "My Universal Credit's not gone in yet. It's due on Thursday. Then I'll go." She looked at me shrewdly. "Have you got kids? I don't think you do. If you did, you'd understand. You'd understand that you'd do anything for them."

"We're not here to talk about me."

"If you had kids, then you'd know. You'd know what it is to be driven up the wall and at the same time, you couldn't be without them." She lowered her voice. "You know, he lies all the time. Only last week he was telling me he'd got three certificates from school and that he'd be on Golden Time on Friday afternoon. On at me to let him take his Nintendo DS into school on Friday, because they can play with their own toys, them that had been good. This was in the same week that I'd had two phone calls off Miss Coates, one to say he'd pushed a kid off a swing, and another saying he'd called her an 'effing bee'. Pardon my language."

"I'm here to help you," I said. "We both want what's best for Jayden, don't we?"

"He doesn't learn it from me, you know," she went on. "I don't know where he gets it. It's like he forgets what he's said. I mean, God knows what he's telling them at school. I've said that to Miss Coates. I've told her, don't you believe a word he says. He makes stuff up." Click of a lighter. Twizzling the blue plastic up and down in her hand, against the sofa arm.

"I don't think our benefits are right," she said, finally. "Can you look into that for us?"

Halimah came in with something that looked like a craft project. Two intersecting balsa wood beams, one horizontal, one vertical, held together by pipe cleaners.

"Here you go, lady," she said. "Made you a present."

Weird thing. I didn't know what it was supposed to be. It had ribbons of different colours hanging all over it. It looked like a cross on Palm Sunday. She brought it over to where I was sitting and nobody else even looked up.

This wasn't even the weirdest thing I'd ever seen in this job. I'd seen all sorts. Six children in a sibling set, all with matching bruises on their left and right thighs in the shape of a remote control, buttons and all. I'd once sat on the floor in a house where the only furniture was an oven, and watched as a Mum laid her baby to sleep wrapped in a blanket, on top of another folded blanket which lay on the kitchenette floor.

"What is it, she says, what is it?" Halimah stood it on the desk, right in my way. I had files stacked up to the level of a mid-height garden wall and here she was adding more problems. "It's a 3D Discrepancy Matrix, isn't it? You fill it in the same way as you would a paper one, only – here." She reached into her cavernous handbag, and pulled out two plastic bags of multicoloured pipe cleaners. "You use these!"

"Hope you didn't pinch these from the supplies cupboard," I said. "Those are for making family trees with the children. Linda would go mad. She's always going on about how expensive they are."

"No." She frowned, as though I'd accused her of defrauding Petty Cash. Everybody here stole stationery. Free post-it notes and pens were one of the few perks in a job where none of us had had a pay rise in eight years. "Went to The Works on my way home yesterday, didn't I? They had late night opening. What's the matter, don't you like it?"

"I love it," I said, although I wasn't sure what mad thought process had led her to bring me it, nor where I was going to keep it. "Thanks, Limah."

"You're welcome," she said, and started looking around for somewhere to sit.

I could write a book about all the things that go wrong with benefits. Their Universal Credit doesn't go in the day it's expected, or the amount is reduced for opaque reasons. A Mum with two children to look after gets six pounds ninety-four to last her two weeks. Sure that it's wrong, that it's not what she was told, she rings the Department for Work and Pensions, spends an hour on the phone, and can't speak to anybody. She gets passed around from department to department. Nobody can help.

"Look," Mrs Wright said, her eyes sliding to the ceiling, "this is stupid. If my benefits were right, you wouldn't even be here."

One of the other stories you hear is of letters appearing from the Jobcentre addressed to the wrong person, sent to the wrong address, with phone numbers on them that don't work. Linda had once tried to implement a system of collating enquiries for the DWP, and doing them all in one go. Naturally, it didn't work. Instead of six people spending an hour on the phone getting nowhere, we had one person spending six hours on the phone getting nowhere. It all worked out to be a very frustrating waste of time.

There was something wrong here, though, I could feel it. An inkling like a spider inside my jumper. She kept on glancing upwards. This was a clue. There could be somebody upstairs. A brother, a stepdad? A mystery man that none of us knew about? Jayden's Dad, she said, was long gone. "We don't see him no more," she said. Jayden's Dad was a bad lot. If Jayden's Dad's new girlfriend ever wondered about his background, she could call in at a police station and ask them about his history, and find out he'd been arrested for domestic violence offences, and two separate judges had given him restraining orders to stop him contacting each of his exes.

"We don't need social services," she said. "What I need is for my Universal Credit to go in on time. How much longer is this going to take?"

She glanced up again. There was somebody upstairs, I was sure of it. Somebody standing very still. Sitting on a bed, perhaps. I wanted to go up and look but I was on my own, and

Linda had been very clear. Nobody goes upstairs in any house if they are a lone worker. You never know what might be up there.

If Tunde hadn't vanished – off sick, I thought, not on holiday; I'd have known if he was going on holiday, because when he went on holiday, he talked about nothing else for weeks beforehand – I would have asked him to come. There would have been two of us then, and one of us could have made an excuse to go upstairs. Asked to use the bathroom. Glanced in all of the doorways up there. Like they say, social workers are sneaky, but I knew, was convinced, that the moment I left the house there would be footsteps. Whoever was hiding up there would stop being so quiet and come downstairs. But there was only one of me, and it wasn't safe to do those kind of exploratory activities when you're alone. We might never know. We'd only find out if Jayden told his teacher that Mum had a boyfriend, but even then, what could we do? It's not a crime for somebody to have a boyfriend.

"I'll give you a referral to the foodbank," I said. "To tide you over."

As I typed my notes, I stuck pipe cleaners to Safiya's model. It was late by the time I got back to the office, after five, and nobody else was there. The duty phones were ringing downstairs. They always rang. It was just that in the daytime, you couldn't hear them over the noise of the office.

Not enough to eat, green pipe cleaner, top right, Known / Certainly True. Trouble with benefits, top right, Known / Certainly True. Looking into benefits wasn't my job, I'd told her that. "Go to your GP," I'd suggested. "Try the One Stop. They'll help you." They wouldn't, but I'd had to say something to get me out of the house. She had kept on saying their only problem was money.

There was somebody else living there, a man we don't know about. Top Left, Not Known / Possibly True. Another thing people say about social workers is that we're nosy, that it's none of our business who Mum goes out with. It's certainly the child's business, and it's the child we're concerned about.

I stopped typing and looked at my model. Two pipe cleaners top right, one pipe cleaner top left. There might be other stuff that I didn't know about, but so long as I didn't know about it, there wasn't enough information for me to do anything. It certainly wasn't enough to meet our criteria for getting involved. Things would have to be so much worse.

I wrote what I knew into the electronic records system, and tentatively marked the case 'to close'. When I next saw Linda, I could discuss it with her.

Then I started peeling the Wrights' pipe cleaners off Halimah's model, and started again with one of Tunde's cases.

Halimah turned in when the model was thick with post-its, and I had fallen asleep with my head on the desk. The office had started to fill up again, but nobody had taken a seat anywhere near me. There was a ring of exclusion around the crazy lady with a Blue Peter craft project and dribble sticking to her face.

"Missus, you should be at home." Her voice was a murmur. "You might think nobody will notice, but they will."

I glanced up dizzily. My laptop was still open, bouncing around a screensaver. *IS IT FRIDAY YET?* I wiped a grubby hand over a grubby cheek and wondered how long it had been since the desk had last been cleaned, what bus-shelter germs were now on my face.

She laid a thick hand on my shoulder. "It won't be long before they all start muttering about you, you know."

"Halimah," I said, "did you ever go to visit a family and think there was somebody else in the house?"

"Wash your face," she said. "Then go home and get changed. It's ok. I'll cover for you." She looked at me, more enquiringly this time. "You know what, you should go home for the rest of the day."

"No way. I've got too much to do."

She dumped her laptop and diary on the desk beside mine. "Well, you'll have to do something, missus. Cancel a few things. Give yourself an easy day." She gave me a good look. "You look like shit. Can't have clients seeing you like that."

"Halimah," I persisted, "I went to see this family yesterday, and I just had this feeling..."

"There was somebody else in the house?" Halimah looked stretched thin, dough being pulled to make a pizza base. She was underbaked, pale as yeast. "Yes, I know. But if they don't tell you, what can you do?"

"Where's Linda?" I was dazed, like I'd been upper-cut punched, the day blurring into grey. Halimah shrugged, motioned for me to pass her the Discrepancy Matrix, and I did.

"I'm putting this away," she said. One of the pipe cleaners fell off it as she walked away. A note fell off, was crushed beneath her blush-toned ballet pump. 'Tunde has signed up to a temp agency,' it said, 'where there's less hassle, and the pay is better.' I had been trying to work out what had happened to him..

Halimah shoved the model into one of the cupboards and said, "Come on lady, wash up, look sharp. Stop messing about if you're going to stay. Make some phone calls. Cancel what you can. Leave early for a change."

I went to school to see Jayden Wright. It was more than was required. It wasn't in the flow chart. If Linda had been around, she'd have told me not to do it. Even Halimah didn't know I was here. I'd told her I was going home.

The head put us in a tiny room the size of a cupboard. Above us, the school motto loomed in multicoloured, threatening optimism. Aspire – Learn – Grow – Be Proud – Achieve!

"How are things at home," I asked, "is anything worrying you?"

His eyes darted like eels in a rock pool. He was a thin boy, wary, with crispbread shoulders. Sitting with him made me want to dig through my purse for old bus tickets, the ones with McDonald's vouchers on the back.

He shook his head, and shrank slightly, hands vanishing into sleeves. The school sweater he wore was worn, frayed around the cuffs. It had been around and around other children, I could see that.

"Miss Coates was a bit worried that you're hungry sometimes," I said. "Do you get enough to eat at home?"

"I'm ok," he said.

Children's lives are small. Think of looking through the wrong end of a telescope, and you'll understand a child's frame of reference. They only know what they know. For all Jayden knew, it was normal to go to bed hungry.

"How's your Mum?" I said. "Is there anybody else living with you?"

He shrunk further. Looked at the floor. His hands, now fully inside the sleeves, vanished like hermit crabs.

When something terrible happens, if a child dies or is shaken to death, all anybody wants to know is: "Why wasn't something done?" and the reason why was sitting in front of me, in a second hand school sweater, lent to him by the Head.

"So, is there anything else you want to tell me?" I said. "I'm here to listen?"

The school bell rang, and his eyes went to the door, then back to me. People tell me I've got a face that makes children want to talk, but this boy was a clam. Either he was used to keeping things shut up, or there were things he'd been told not to say.

Out in the rest of the school, chairs scraped across the floor, children yelped and laughed. The corridor filled with a golden rhombus of light as a door to the playground opened.

"Off you go," I said, "Thanks for coming to see me."

I got the family a referral to a food bank, and marked the case 'to close'. A dozen other bruised and hungry children were waiting, plus a few of Tunde's cases, which had been reassigned to me.

Halimah seemed to be there for the long haul. There was plenty to do and not enough of us to do it. She worked her own cases, a few of Tunde's, plus a few from those social workers who went off sick, and all day long we both made phone calls and knocked at doors that went unanswered.

The Discrepancy Matrix, I put in the little kitchen, on the tea tray by the kettle. People played with it whilst they waited for the kettle to boil. They wrote each other encouraging notes like, "Proud To Work In The Best Social Work Team In The City!" and "You're not in the gutter, you've got a front row seat for staring at the stars" and "Good Luck, Dave!" and "Please wash your teaspoons."

On my birthday, I called in at Morrison's to get a chocolate cake. It was a rich diabetic nightmare twice the size of my own head. "There she is," Halimah said when I arrived. There was no hiding with a cake this size. They'd given it to me in a carton with a see-through lid. "How old are you this time? Twenty-four?"

"And the rest," I said.

Everybody else in the office watched me walk by with this cake, and pretended not to, cats watching sparrows in a bird bath. Any moment they'd finish their phone calls and their notes and descend, tearing me limb from limb, my frail skeleton lying forgotten on the kitchenette lino whilst they got stuck into the rich fudge icing. We were getting smaller. We had once been twenty, then sixteen, and now twelve. We hovered around a dozen and couldn't get above it. I hadn't seen Linda in months.

"Come on then lady, get into it," Halimah said. "Don't make us all wait." She hovered, scraping through a straw-bale of unwashed cutlery to try and find a knife. "Every now and then it's good to have cake for breakfast," she said, "don't you think?"

I did think, but my skin was turning grey. Sometimes I looked at myself in the mirror and wondered what had happened. There were bags under my eyes that you could have kept returning to use for your shopping for years. *A person is not supposed to get by on sugar and caffeine*, that was what the state of my skin said. I kept telling myself I was going to start bringing an apple to work every day, and that I was going to have salad for lunch instead of chips. In reality, what happened was that I brought an apple to work every day, then usually brought it home again, knocking around in the bottom of my bag. I took the apple for a walk like this every day, and then when it was more bruised than a boxer, I'd take it out and throw it away.

"Alright," I said. "Let me go and call them in." My mobile flashed on the desk: *Happy birthday! From your friend Tunde :-)*

I picked it up, and shouted: "It's my birthday!" in a general sort of way.

Heads rose from laptops. There was a smile or two. The social work student in the corner, pink-faced and optimistic, shook her head, peacock-feather earrings flickering. "Not for me," she said. "I'm trying to be good."

"How old," Dave shouted, "not you, the cake?"

"Twenty-one," I said. "It's very mature."

"There's a joke in there somewhere," he replied.

What happened to you? I wrote back. *You just disappeared one day without saying goodbye?*

In the kitchenette, Halimah was waiting. She had found a serrated knife and was cutting ugly slices from the cake. In her hands it became churned mud. "I'm making a real mess of this," she said. "Should have left it to you." The knife wasn't up to the job; it couldn't even reach to the centre of the cake. Her fingers were covered.

"Never mind." Reaching over her to get to the Discrepancy Matrix, I looked for the right message, then found it in the top right-hand quadrant, close to where the axes met. "Here, Halimah, this is for you," I said. "You Can Do It!" it said. "You Are Amazing!"

TOP DOG

Sleep came sparingly that first week. Dozing evenings, Lucas heard Lilla and Peepers moving around in the room upstairs. He often woke again when it was dark, hearing the sound of twigs tapping the glass. It made him lousy. What must his housemates think of him, knackered, and too worn out to do any of the things they'd brought him in for? Nobody said anything, but he knew they must think it.

It had a long list, the housing co-op. People wanted in for the security and cheap rent; for the knowledge that you weren't necessarily thrown out for not paying. Lucas had vaulted them all with his promise to be handy around the house. "I've got all of my own tools," he'd said. Yet now, instead of putting them to use, he spent his afternoons laying on the bed, looking at the insides of his own eyelids, and trying not to think about Shelley being on her own in the flat.

In the mornings, he walked the postal route, eyes half-closed, muddling the house numbers. A fat-calved woman came thundering out of 8 Carson Avenue to complain about having her neighbours' mail. "It's not *my* birthday," she said. Lonely, he thought, and with nothing better to do than argue with the postman.

Down by the telephone exchange he discovered a dog. It was an old thing with brindle patches, and a grey whiskered muzzle. The early morning mist clung to its bony haunches. "Come, come boy," he said. He reached down to it and the dog, giving him a desperate look, cowered away. Lucas bundled him up, put him in the mail sack, and carried him around the rest of the route. "I will call you Bogle," he said, as he pushed envelopes through the doors. "And you can come live with me in my little corner of Anarchist utopia."

When he arrived home, there was a welt in his shoulder from carrying the sack, and his other housemate Yeurtes was waiting in the hallway. He took one look at the dog and said: "You ought to have called a meeting first."

Lucas said, "Sorry." He took the dog upstairs and gave it some biscuits. It sniffed them mournfully and chewed a small mouthful for a long time. Then it sighed, lay its head between its paws, and looked sadly at the rest of the food in the bowl.

"I'm going to set up the radio, Bogle," Lucas said. He crouched and shook the receiver gently. The afternoon news came in and out of focus, like a ship passing through heavy fog. "Once I get this working," he said to the dog, "you and me will be able to listen to Woman's Hour." The dog resettled his head and looked at him sideways. "Don't look at me like that," Lucas said. "This is the first day of the rest of our lives."

There was a knock. Lilla came in, wearing a washed-out clown outfit, and carrying a tennis ball. "I've heard we've got a new housemate," she said. She rolled the ball along the floor and the dog watched it pass, closing his eyes as it settled into the corner.

"I think he's pretty old," Lucas said. With the door open, he could smell the damp from the hallway carpet.

"All the same," she said, scratching the mutt between the ears, "this is a good dog."

Letting go of the transistor, Lucas tapped the lid. The fizzing stopped. "There," he said. "Yeurtes said I had to call a meeting about keeping a pet."

"Let me tell you a secret," Lilla said. She rubbed Bogle's side. He yawned, and a musical squeak came out. "Yeurtes *loves* dogs. Don't worry about it." She stood. "Well, it's my turn to cook. See you for dinner." She went out.

Lucas stood by the stereo and looked at the bare room. The dog and the radio were the only things interrupting the long lines of the floorboards. Fleas or not, it seemed cruel to make the brute sleep on the floor. He sat on the bed, slapping his thighs gently. "Come up," he said. "Come, boy." Bogle watched, as though not knowing what welcome meant. "Never mind," Lucas said. "You rest. I'm going to have a look at those shelves."

He went and got the stepladder out of the utility closet. Here he was, fixing shelves for three virtual strangers, and still not knowing where things had gone wrong. A year of sofa cuddling and Shelley had suddenly gone quiet, wearing a look like she was in the distance. The end had come, as he'd known it would – he'd been bracing himself for it – and she'd said: "Don't feel that you have to move out. You can sleep on the sofa as long as you like." It had left him reeling, and wondering why, when she no longer wanted to be together, she was being so kind?

Peepers was sitting in the living room window, the last of the ebbing light landing on his shoulders. In the alcove beside him the shelves bowed. Books slid down the gaps at either end. "Alright if I start work on these?" Lucas said.

"Yes," said Peepers, leaping up. "I'll help."

Lucas looked at the jumble. A novella had forced itself a new home between a dictionary's leaves. Radical gardening pamphlets were squeezed together like takeaway menus. In trying to save the earth, the housemates had used whatever reclaimed wood they could find and ended up with this mess. The shelves were too short and had no support in the middle. Never mind: it was easily fixed. He tapped the tape measure against his leg and felt the familiar excitement that came with the prospect of cleaning up a mess. "Here," he said. "I'll show you how to measure up."

"Sure." Peepers put his book down on the chair arm. "Take the books off first?" He was up the steps, handing them down an armful at a time. "Careful when you come in, Lilla," he called through the kitchen arch. "We've got books all over the floor in here."

The front door opened, and Lucas paused. He heard a quiet metallic jingle in the hall. Then the sound of Bogle coming down the stairs in a slow, arthritic thump, one step at a time.

Yeurtes was standing by the front door, a chain-linked dog lead in his back hand. "Now look, I don't want to pre-empt tonight's discussion," he said, waving his big, bear-like arms. "So don't take this as an indication of my opinion one way or the other." Standing by the foot of the stairs, Bogle wagged his tail slowly. "But I found this lead in a skip and thought that if the house meeting decided that the dog was allowed to stay..." He trailed off, lifting the hand holding the lead.

"If," said Peepers. He twisted around to Lucas, winking. "*If.*"

Lucas had never had a pet. Not even an old, ailing one like this, one close to coughing its last breath. His old landlord said that their fur and claws ruined the furniture – in a house where the sofa looked like it had already been through a house fire.

Loping into the room, the dog settled its hind legs down by the bookshelves and looked up at Lucas expectantly. Walking around the table, he scratched it behind the ears. "It looks like you might be able to stay," he said. "You lucky, lucky thing."

Lilla suggested that Bogle could be a working dog. Earn his place by mousing the vermin or keeping out intruders. But the dog had a clement temperament and was not good for either. He allowed mice to run over and around him, and hardly noticed even when they scampered over his paws. Strangers to the house were greeted with a sad look, and a resigned whimper; a combination that said, "Why are you in my seat?"

Lucas took the dog with him to work. He was spending too long in his thoughts and liked to have the company. It was a good way, he'd decided, for it to get the daily exercise it needed.

Taking the hound slowed him. For one thing, it couldn't go any quicker than its rheumatic joints, and for another, it was a nice dog, and people would stop to pet it. He met a lot of women that way. Even joggers would slow, come to a stop, and scratch Bogle's thin head. "What's his name?" they'd say.

"Now you are really earning your keep," Lucas would say, after another smile from a pink-flushed lady in Lycra.

They were coming out of Carson Close one morning, when Lucas saw a woman half-chasing down the street after three dogs. There were two tan spaniels and a blotched one, all tongues lolling. Bogle leapt forward, tugging at his collar. His tail whipped hard against Lucas' leg. It was the only time Lucas had ever known him excited. He had no idea the old man could be so strong; it left a burn in his palm. "Steady on," he said.

The woman laughed on her way past. The sun caught her eyes like light landing on the sea. "Bet he keeps you busy," she said. She went by, in the direction of the park.

Lucas decided that it wouldn't kill the occupants of Carson Drive to not get their bills for another hour. "Come on, Bogle," he said. The two of them ran down the road after Bogle's new friends.

The park lay behind a short stone wall. Beyond a square of grass used by the local boys for cricket was a bench, and after that a slope of dandelions and wildflowers. Lucas took up a spot on the seat and watched the spaniels gambol on the hill.

Bogle lay in a patch of daisies, legs folded under him. The younger dogs ran for sticks, darting past with their ears flowing in the wind. The old professor looked like he was having the time of his life.

The woman was standing under a tree, the shade speckling her broad face. She was older than he'd first thought, he saw, with a wedding ring on her left hand. "Oh well," he said. She was throwing treats, the dogs snuffling the ground for them. He watched the blotched dog snout the earth. When it moved away, he saw a familiar head behind the stalks. Blonde, unkempt, and smiling at somebody lying on the ground beside her.

He stopped himself from calling out. It was none of his business now, where Shelley went, and what she did. Hand in pocket, fingers touching the edge of the kibbled dog treats, Lucas kept staring, looking for the other head to rise. He wondered who it was and waited for the sting to start.

Bogle appeared, putting his jaw on Lucas' knee. His eyes contained a world of sadness; an expression that disappeared as soon as the biscuits came out. Lucas let him lick them from his palm and glanced at the top of Shelley's head. She was giggling in a way he hadn't seen since the day they'd first gone out. Seeing her so different like that – it was like looking at a stranger.

The dog harrumphed, tacking its paws on the concrete. "I know, dog," he said. "We'll go and do the rest of the post soon." Bogle set his nose to sniffing Lucas' trouser pocket. "You've had your lot," Lucas said.

He looked again, saw her face disappear downwards. The sight of the green made him think about the garden at home, about Lilla's raspberry canes fruiting at the front of the house. More would be ready for picking today, hot pink and ripe, perfect for fruit crumble. The dog licked his trousers, leaving a trail of damp over his knee. "Man's best friend, eh?" he said, trying to wipe it dry. It was no use: the trail was already setting, and the trousers would need to go in the wash. "Couldn't have brought you home if I'd been in the flat, could I?" Lucas scratched the lone triangle of fluff behind Bogle's left ear and thought about rigging up a clothes drier. A wooden one that could lift by a pulley away from the floor, and stop the mice making nests of their drying clothes. "Come on, beast," he said, getting up. "You and I have got work to do."

GENUS

My brother was born strange. As a child, he spent hours gazing into the distance, clenching and tapping his fingers, when he was supposed to be minding the seedlings.

You only had to walk one end of the greenhouse to the other, taking the watering can in hand. You gave every tray a sprinkle, more if the earth was dry. Each day the seedlings grew a little; it was part of the job to keep an eye on them, see whether they had grown big enough to go out into the furrows outside. I'd been doing it myself since I was six, and tall enough just to see over the shelves. But my brother, though he had been doing it longer, did it poorly. He would put the can down at the end of the hut and look out of the window, mouthing words as if there were somebody standing on the other side – somebody none of the rest of us could see.

On her bad days, my mother used to call John 'a liability'. There were only four of us, and we all had to contribute something to keep the crops going. Twice a day around the glass houses wasn't a lot to ask. But he couldn't manage that, or be relied upon to run the trades down into the village either. He'd take the bicycle out and come back with the basket empty, and all that somehow without getting the vegetables to the people who needed them. We'd run short after needing to send two second bags after the missing first bags, and that gave us all a few thin years: us up on the land, and those down in the valley alike. Once he'd cost everybody enough like this a few times, we stopped putting him to work altogether.

There was an elderly couple on the land beside us. Gramma Phoebe and Gramps Thompson, we called them, although we were by no way related. The land on which the farm stood had once been a car park. A few years after the collapse, in the days when *he* had been a teenager, there started to be enough earth to use to grow crops. Gramps Thompson liked to remember those stories to us; he said it was the only way he could work the farm, now his body was getting stiff.

It fell to me to take John's share. By doing that, I learned the whole trade of the farm, from germination to harvest, and everything in between, companion planting and rotation and such. It looks so easy when you begin, the green tips coming up out of the earth; a stranger visiting might not realise how much work there is in it. If you didn't know, you might make the mistake of thinking that the plants would come up by themselves.

We buried Gramma and Gramps when I was fourteen, and not long after, two thin and very earnest men moved into their old cottage, while mother and father went away on their bicycles to travel the world. Mother said: "You're old enough now to manage." She tied a scarf over her hair, and went away ringing her bicycle bell, like there might be something around the next corner.

The two new men were called Elliot and Davis. They each wore black all the time and took the whole thing as seriously as death. Put their hoes into the ground like they thought they were starting a whole new world. They had been building before they came to us, and it was convenient to have them, since our old shack was coming apart at the seams, and I hardly knew what to do. When the wind blew at night, I could see stars through the cracks in the roof.

We were in the third year of a five-year crop rotation then, and the beds in front of the houses were all potatoes. In the two long beds beyond were alliums – leeks and onions. Cabbage was popular in the village – it was all some of my neighbours ate – so I had done a whole bed of those. Nobody went in for kale much, but it was an easier grow than cabbage, and I hoped to get it popular.

When we cut the cabbages, I said to Davis to mind the ones marked off with red twine, for those were the keepers. Every year, I left a dozen in the ground to go to seed, and then we'd gather that to grow the same type again next year. It was the same as farmers had always done, like my father had taught me, and like Gramps had taught him before I came along.

"I see," Davis said, his face like the granite overhang, and I really do think that if he'd had a pencil to hand, he would have written it down.

Elliot hammered all the weak points in the house together, and my brother, well, I didn't know where he was. John was given to disappearing for days at a time and I didn't bother myself about where. If he happened to be home at dinnertime, we'd give him a bowl of something to eat, and if he wasn't, we'd eat it all ourselves.

After dinner one night, I showed Elliot and Davis my diagrams. A drawing of the whole planting area, glass house included, with the months for planting and harvest written down one side. The brewery down in the valley had traded us a case of beer, and I was getting relaxed on it.

"Successive planting," I said, "is the key to continual harvesting." I drew a grid down one side, with columns for germination, planting out, and harvest. "And even so, this is only a rough guide. You always have to keep an eye on the weather." A late frost could do for all your hard work, and leave everybody hungry. It was a farmer's responsibility to wait until it was truly safe to plant out.

"Last year," I said, and I was really enjoying the beer by that time, "we got no beer at all. All the blackberries were fruiting, but I hadn't the time to pick the fruit and send it down into the valley. I was as good as on my own up here."

Davis put his bottle down. "John ought to be doing his share of the work," he said. "What does he do all day, anyway?"

I paused, leaning over the sketch, retracing the word 'broccoli'. I found that I did not know the answer to the question. John's idleness had become such a matter of fact, that it had hardly occurred to me to try to change it. "He's always been like this," I said. "Since we were children. The thing you have to understand is, John wasn't built for work."

"Then we're carrying him," he said. "We're doing his share of the work, for him to get all the benefits. How do you call that fair?"

Elliot shushed him. "It doesn't make any difference to the amount of work, surely," he said. "We'd have to do it whether John were here or not."

"But if he *wasn't*," Davis continued, his finger tapping at the tabletop like a dull hammer, "We could make space for somebody who would contribute something." He stretched his arms out. "I'm thinking mainly of you, Ellen. You look tired. Doesn't she?"

I put my beer down on the table, reluctantly, thinking about the second watering still to do. "I don't know, Davis," I said. "It's hard work teaching the farm to new people."

It didn't seem much to me like it was a burden to have John around. If he was kept out of the work, he did no harm, and didn't haul us backward. What Davis didn't understand was that there were things about my brother that made him different, things you couldn't shake out of him by trying to make him behave.

"There's a second watering to do tonight," I said. "Will one of you help me with it?"

The glass houses were up on the hill, where Gramma had put them to get the best light. There were leeks still in, long tops growing up like thick grass. The sweetcorn was still closed, its white-translucent skin catching remnants of the sun. Elliot went out with me across the land.

As we walked by the allium bed, I saw dozens of leeks trampled. Their leaves crushed and bent, a fresh onion smell coming strongly from the earth. Between the hammered plants was a man's footprint.

His hand rested a second on my shoulder. "There," Elliot said, pointing up at the glass house.

There was a dark shape behind the glass. "That's John," I said. His hands were busy in the earth.

"Quickly," he said.

John was at the lettuce trays when we got to him. Had them three deep in front of him, nipping out the leaves. A dozen trays were ruined already. Torn seedlings lay on the tops.

He was muttering: "Best bred and smart genes. Best bred. Best bred."

Those lettuces were the only seedlings we had for winter, and it was too late to start more. I pulled the tray away from him. "This is November's crop you're killing," I shouted. "What are you doing?"

Around his eyes I saw red. "I'm saving us from your mistakes," he said, and he went on making the kill motions in the air, even though the tray had been taken away.

"What's wrong with you?" I said. "You can't destroy the plants like this."

"Best bred. All changed genes, for disease resistance and uniformity of colour, and what else?" he rambled. "Breed out one trait, and what goes with it? And what bring? We don't know that it's safe. We could all get sick if we don't stop it now. Somebody has to do something. Somebody has to stop it." He was already turning away.

I couldn't get to him fast enough. There was nowhere to put the trays I'd already taken, so I put them on the shelf. "Stop it, John. You don't know what you're talking about."

"It changes them, on the inside. In ways that you can't see. The breeding. They're inventions, and you can't stop the change. It'll spread everywhere – to every farm. Pollen can travel a hundred miles on a bee's leg."

It was Elliot, not me, who made him stop, grabbing him by the wrists with his long workman's fingers. "That's enough. We can't do without this year's crops. Now stop it."

John looked at him, jaw slack, eyes wide, like he was just seeing Elliot for the first time. "What's your name, again?"

I looked beyond them at the broccoli. All twenty trays of it all stalk now, no leaves. I dreaded to think what else John would do if left here alone.

"Would you go into the house, John?" I said. "Davis made a stew and there's plenty over. You haven't done a thing on the farm all summer. Now would you just do me this one thing?"

"For you," he said, although his face was like a stranger's.

Elliot was already reaching for the watering can as we passed. "Get Davis to bring some bedding out," he said. "I'll sleep across the door tonight."

Davis and I put my brother down in my parents' old bed, and tightened the sheets so he couldn't get out again. We took turns to sleep in a rocking chair in the doorway, the aim being that we should talk John back into bed should he manage to wriggle free. My turn was between midnight and four, and I didn't get a wink. The wood was hard, and I was in no position to sleep. I only ever dozed and would have been useless at anything besides going back to sleep myself if John ever had roused.

When Davis came at four, I thought I saw a shooting star. "You go and get some decent sleep," he said.

I was awake again two hours later and wondering what to do. There weren't enough of us for somebody to stay with John all day. I looked through my half open door and saw Elliot, covered in a fine coating of earth all down one side. Then the rocking chair creaked, and he turned and said a few words, and I knew then that Davis was awake too.

My brother was still sleeping when we ate.

"I think I know some people who could look after John." Elliot had cleaned his face, and was sitting with his hand on Davis', as was his habit. "Kind people, caregivers, up there in the woods. I can ride up there and ask them to come see about him."

I was still wrapped in the blanket. Holding it so tight I had almost crushed it to tissue. "What do you mean?"

Elliot said gently, "He's not right, Ellen. And we can't look after him here – not with the farm to manage. Imagine having to keep watch over him every single night. We can't do it."

I got up, pulled off my nightgown and put on my trousers, even though they were both there looking. We were already late starting. The sun was up, and soon it would be too hot to weed. Water poured on the trays any later than this would turn to steam as soon as it hit the compost – unless it had already been done.

"Did you water the plants before you came down?" I asked.

Elliot nodded. "For what good it'll do."

Hearing him say it made real what we had already lost. Things that could not be replaced, and it being much too late in the year for them to be resown. And my brother there in the bed, and us unable to look after him the way he needed it. I held my face in my hands, and had a little weep. I thought: *I'll give myself five minutes to do it, then get on with what has to be done.*

A hand on my arm. Davis' hand, with the square, stubby palm, the dry skin. I felt him crouch beside me. "Why don't you take the day off?"

I said, "It'll set us further back." Besides, I needed something to think about, though this I did not say.

"Should we send Elliot on up to the place in the woods?" Davis said: "Don't worry about John. He'll sleep."

I went out into the fields. There were things to do. I started by digging out the leeks, to see what of those could be salvaged. They were spindly yet, and now would never grow any; but there were also a few, if cut below the footprint, that would do for soup. I pulled those out and put them into a truckle.

The sun was slipping from its highest point, when I heard the grind of cranks. For hours, I had done nothing myself besides sit on the edge of the leek bed. I was holding one of the broken plants, looking down at the mud between the rings, and thinking about how it would be too gritty for eating. I was remembering how mother used to slide the outer rings off and wash the earth away in a bucket.

Davis was working his hoe around the raised beds. He called, "Hello!"

They were coming up the hill brow, Elliot and two others. A tall man with sinewy arms, and a younger woman with short hair. They were cycling a contraption with two bikes, and something like a low-sided caravan behind it.

Davis left off his work. The woman started pulling buckles and straps out over the trailer sides. When my shadow fell over her, she said, "Now don't be alarmed. The buckles and such are just for his safety." There were cushions inside, their covers worn partly away.

"Johann," said the man. I shook hands with him. He had a firm grip, and as he let go, I remember thinking that he'd spend the next day or so smelling strongly of onions. "And this here's Kate. Elliot tells us that all is not well with your brother."

Kate got to her feet, squinting. The sun was shining right into her eyes, and her hair looked like it had been cut with something blunt.

"He's always been odd," I said. "But last night was something else."

I looked at Johann fully, and saw a greyness around his eyes, as though they'd been powdered in ash. "In what way?" he said.

"He was in there." I pointed up the hill. "Pulling next year's seedlings out of the ground and talking all kinds of—" It felt like I was betraying my brother by saying so, and I added: "It was like he thought the plants could kill us. I've never known him like that before."

She and Johann glanced at one another.

"Are you frightened of him?" Kate said.

"No," I said, just as Davis added:

"We had to watch over him all night. We were afraid he would get up again and do more damage."

Johann said: "Does he ever wander off?"

I thought of the weeks, for days at a time, where John would be gone. Off without saying a word, and none of us knowing when he would return. Those were long nights of beer and laughter, and of planning the work day as we liked. And sometimes sitting on the edge of a chair, waiting for the click of the door to say he was back. The way he would sit in long silence in another room, darkening everything. A part of me wished that he would stay away.

"Sometimes," I said. "But—"

Shouting. John was awake and carrying on. "They're casting a rod over nature. Making us pay for a thing that belongs to us all!"

"Is that him?" Johann said.

I nodded. "He's got this idea in his head about the seeds. Seems to think they're not a natural carry-over from last year – almost like he believes I got them from somewhere. I don't know where he got the idea. We save the seeds ourselves, from season to season."

There was the sound of sheets tearing, and an enraged howl, like a trapped fox. As the cotton ripped, I remembered the good sheets were on John's bed. No longer now: probably in ribbons, ruined for good.

Davis darted into the house. "I'll see to him," he said.

Johann put a hand on my arm. "Your brother believes things that aren't true," he said. "We've seen it before, in the others we look after."

Kate said, "How many does this farm feed?"

A commotion, and both John and Davis came to the door. John was red-faced and slavering at the mouth. Davis' nose was bleeding. "I'm sorry," he said. "I tried to stop him."

"You can't keep me a prisoner," John said, his hands clenching and unclenching. "I'm not your property."

I turned to Kate and said: "Are you sure you can look after him?" I wouldn't have liked to try and get him on a bike now, not looking the way he did – fierce and fit to swing for anybody.

"John." Johann's voice softened. He led my brother across to the trailer. It was like witchcraft, the way John followed him, all of a sudden like a pet lamb.

"Don't worry," Kate said, "We've got another lad just like him. We're used to it. We've got a wind-up record player at the house, and musical instruments that the residents use. There's a library and a garden. Lots of therapeutic activities he could do. He'll be well looked after." I looked at her, this stranger with flecks of gold in her eyes, her heavy arms and legs, and wondered for a moment who she was.

Davis was clutching a torn piece from the bedclothes. It was red with his blood, and dripping. No amount of washing would make that come out.

Johann had already got my brother into the trailer. I don't know how he managed to get him to move so fast – nobody had ever been able to get John to obey them like that, not even my mother and father. He was strapped down, with a heavy looking buckle over his lap, and a wide grin over his face.

Just then I heard the tower bells. They hadn't rung in a long while, and they were tolling now to signal an evening of dancing in the brewery tap. It had been a while since I'd been to a party. I'd missed the last one, and the one before that. There always seemed to be too much to do for me to go down into the village.

"Can I come and visit him?" I said.

She turned and glanced at Johann. He was over by the wall, trying to pet the local mousing cat. It was a scrawny, vicious thing, and nobody could get anywhere near it. But Johann had a finger under its chin, and it was tipping its head all the way back.

"Give him a week or two to settle in," she said, and then she and Johann got onto the contraption, and pedalled away.

I watched their shadows run jaggedly over the stone wall and gate, heard John's whoop shrink into the distance. My brother had been gone many long periods, but this time felt different. He would not be coming back. I knew it as I watched the cart disappear around the corner.

We spent a lot of evenings that summer out on the porch. Davis' nose went back to its normal shape some time around midsummer, and we talked late into every night. It wasn't that we were carousing. It was that we'd found a way to enjoy ourselves.

In the late nights, I would sometimes think about John, and feel bad for having sent him away. Elliot and Davis both told me not to fret, and that we should think of finding a fourth person. "But not yet," they said. "Not when things are going so well." And we would clink our glasses together, and I would talk some more about how I ought to go and visit my brother.

It went on like that some months, and it was only when the onion tops dropped, and the chill came in the air, that I thought that I perhaps had left it too long. "He'll think I've abandoned him," I started to say.

We brought the harvest fully in, and I started to think that it was time for me to go. For that was the quiet time of year, once the pickling and bottling were done.

Nobody had set a price for minding John, but when I thought about it, I saw how much more we'd accomplished with him gone. There were endless carrots in the tin baths, more cabbages than we could ever pickle. It was worth a lot to us, and those down in the village, to not have him burden us.

So setting out, I packed a trailer full. Gramma Phoebe had used to say that when she'd been young, if you had a job you could buy anything you could afford with the money they paid you to do it. When the whole system had gone wrong, people weren't getting paid for their work – which in any case hardly mattered, since the shops no longer had anything on their shelves. People were standing around in the streets with piles of paper money that was hardly worth even lighting on fire. There was unrest, and two of Gramma's best friends died. Afterwards, Gramma Phoebe mistrusted any trade that didn't involve the exchange of actual goods. She'd trade nothing if not for something she could hold in her hand. It was a rule to which we'd held fast at the farm ever since.

Though Elliot and Davis both said they would come if I wished, I instead asked Elliot to draw a map so that I could go on my own. It seemed to me it might upset my brother to have too many visitors at the one time. I fixed the cart to Elliot's silver cruiser and set out.

It was a two hour ride either way, and I did not ride long distances often. This was only the second time I'd gone anywhere since taking the farm over myself. I was wrapped up in gloves and a heavy cardigan, and already overheated by the time I got to the old bank.

From there led the road up to the cottage. It was not one much used. The ancient tarmac had survived all these years. Riding Elliot's bike over it was like sitting in a boat on a calm lake. Perfectly smooth, like nothing I'd ever felt before. The road circled a point, always pressing right, clinging to the hill in a spiral. The further I climbed, the more evidence of life I heard. A steady clang, like a blacksmith at an anvil. Sometimes a single voice, singing. And then the road straightened, and at the end of it I saw a stone cottage. It was low and small-windowed, with a field of stubby hay-stalks in front, cut short and all burned black. There was the smell of torched rubber in the air.

"This is my house," I heard a man shout, "and I do what I want." I couldn't see the owner of the voice. It wasn't John, although that sounded like something John would say.

Panes at the house front were broken, I noticed, and as I reached the fence, Kate stumbled out of the front door. I leaned Elliot's bike against the post and saw that she had a black eye.

"Everybody, gather round." A second voice, sounding high and urgent – my brother, sounding panicked. "We all need to stay away from Lewis. He's being anti-social."

"Hello," Kate said, and she winched up a smile. "I've been telling him you'd come soon."

Something smashed, maybe pottery or plates, but not glass. "I do what I like," the first voice said.

Another man came out. Young, thin and pale, like a seedling kept too long out of the light. He was all skin and elbows, and his clothes wore him, awkwardly. He looked too afraid to come over. This boy too, I thought, was somebody's brother.

"Don't worry about the noise," she said. "It's not like this all the time. It just happens that you've caught us—" More things broken, the sound of clay shattering on a stone floor. "...and you'll be able to go in in a minute."

Though she'd said not to worry about the noise, I found I couldn't much help it. My brother was in the kitchen, pacing back and forth between the two broken windows. He looked much older than when he had left us, and was wearing a heavy wax jacket, a thing that looked like it was meant for deep winter. I didn't recognise it, nor know where it had come from. "Is it just you and Johann here?" I asked. "With all of the..."

"Well, there's three of us," she said. "Me, Johann and Carlos. It's tough work. Not many stick it out." She glanced over at the trailer. "Hey, are those cabbages?"

"I brought them for you," I said. "To say thanks."

"That's kind. Isn't that kind, Jem?"

There was a yelp, and a dreadful grinding, like a large and rusty bike chain. A rush of pressured water, and then a scream, like fighting cats. The voice ebbed to a moan, and then a whimper, and then it, like the hose, stopped.

"There," she said. "That's him out the back. You'll be able to go in now."

My brother came around the side of the house, grinning. His hair was all sticking up in front, and his shoes were wet. When he saw me, he broke into a trot. "Don't you just love this place?" he said. "Listen to the birdsong!"

I listened, but all I could hear was the sound of my own guilt. There was cruelty here, and my brother was a part of it.

"You just hosed somebody," I said, hearing myself as if through somebody else's ears. It was the sound of Gramma Phoebe's voice.

"That's right," he said, clapping me sturdily on the shoulder. "It's in the rules. We all agreed to it at a house meeting. Been hosed myself, plenty of times."

Kate looked at me and shrugged. "I know it sounds bad," she said, "But everybody agreed. And it's the quickest way to calm down, sometimes." She pointed him around to the trailer. "Look what your sister brought."

He looked, and his face darkened. "I won't eat those." There was the look of a storm on his face now, like we'd hear thunder any moment. "They're poison." He turned, and strode back to the house, slamming the door behind him. The top part of the living room window slid out, and smashed on the ground.

I remembered then, all about him. Having come here hoping to find him bettered, I'd instead found him as he always was, only a little older.

Jem was over at the trailer, a wicker basket over each arm. He was lifting the cabbages out, one heavy head at a time.

Kate yawned, and I looked up at the cottage, wondering which was her room. They must all bed somewhere upstairs, she and Johann and Carlos and all of the distressed men who called it home, shouting and yowling the whole night through. I wondered whether she ever got any rest.

"This was the kindest thing you could do for your brother," she said. "See to it that he eats well. These," – she lifted a bunch of carrots – "will look the same as any other once they're in a stew."

I nodded and went into the house to find him. The inside was dark, with a low ceiling and white walls; I noticed that a lot of the furniture was broken.

He was shut up in the first room. I settled on the top step, listening to Johann and another man tidying up downstairs in the kitchen.

"It's a shame about these plates," Johann was saying. "But you know what? We could use the broken pieces to make a mosaic."

The other man helping was very taken with this idea. "Yes. To decorate the bathroom."

There was no puddle on the landing carpet, no run of water spots up the stairs. The wet man had never left the downstairs of the house. He was down in the kitchen, sweeping up.

I sat with my shoulder up against the door, thinking about the way we had strapped John down to my mother's bed. How panic had fluttered as I'd tucked the white ends under the mattress, fretting about what on earth to do. Not just for that day, but for the days and weeks coming. I'd thought seasons ahead, like I always did. And now here we were.

Since I didn't know what to say to my brother, I said nothing. Seemed to me like any words that crossed my mouth could only make things worse, anyhow. News of the farm wouldn't cheer him. Any thought of inviting him back for a visit I'd brushed out of mind. It wouldn't make him happy, not with him believing what he did. And yet I hated to leave him here, in this place. Where my permission had brought him, to this falling-down place, with its smashed windows, its furniture that was no more than sticks and thread.

Kate shouted up the stairs that I could stay for dinner, but I hardly saw how that could help. For John to have me sitting across the table from him when he was already angry, and not likely to calm down any time soon.

"They all get upset when family visit," she said. "Don't blame yourself."

Ribbons of bright green cabbage on the cutting board, and even the hosed man, dry now, and laughing. The smell of onions frying in a crock pot.

"I'm fine," I said, because once I'd gone down to the kitchen, I could see how the dark was falling, and how hard it might be to find my way back. "Thanks for looking after him."

There was a lightness to the bike, with the vegetables all gone from the trailer. It span down the hillside, wheels singing. I was at the foot of the hill much sooner than I thought.

Somebody had pushed the door almost closed at the old bank. It rested almost in the frame, piles of curled red leaves up against its foot. Though it was not much cold yet, somebody had a fire lit. The smoke was on the air — the smell of fallen willow, with meat being cooked on a spit — rabbit, I thought. Being able to smell it made me hungry on my own account.

Elliot and Davis had kept me over a large bowl of soup, and there was a chew of spelt bread from the baker.

"How was he?" Davis asked.

For a moment, with the taste of leek and thyme in my mouth, I was lost for a way to describe it all.

"Fine," I said. "He likes it there. Says it's very peaceful." I didn't say a thing about the windows, or the man who had broken every plate.

"Good," he said. "Good." He and Elliot were holding hands on the tabletop.

"Don't they do an amazing job up there?" Elliot said. "I don't know what we'd do if any of the caregivers decided they didn't want to do it anymore."

"They're good people alright," Davis said, "having the calling to do work like that."

There was something very satisfying in the last few mouthfuls of soup. I felt myself full-bellied and content. "They are."

"Well," Elliot said, "then that's that." He stood up from the table, and he and Davis both went to turn in.

The house was full of a beautiful silence. I went on sitting in the chair a long time, enjoying it. The way the new roof held and settled, without creaking. That there was no danger of hearing the door suddenly open and seeing my brother there by it. I looked at the cupboards, with their sturdy knobs, and imagined I could hear a long, slow, wooden heartbeat.

On the way to my own bed, I passed my brother's. It was empty now, nothing in it but the mattress, and the low table on one side. Elliot was keeping it swept, though it had not been slept in for a long time. As I came by, I closed the door, pulling the handle until I felt it click. It wasn't until I was absolutely sure that the room was good and solid shut, that it really wouldn't come open again, that I left the place alone.

MAPS OF IMAGINARY TOWNS

Hollis could say that his was a happy childhood, up to a point. Mother, father, older brother: things exactly as they were supposed to be. Dad went to work every day in one of three grey suits: going to the factory offices, and never coming home with his hands dirty.

Ten minutes before Hollis and Gordon went to catch the bus, the same things happened every day. Dad ruffled their heads, said: "Ta-ra, lads," kissed Ma on the cheek, then went out in his coat and hat, carrying his briefcase.

One corner of the garden was his and Gordon's own. It was the place they played Terror, shooting one another with sticks for guns. Over the tops of felled logs and loose fence panels. Muddy in those trenches they'd dug, only knowing it was time to come in when Ma called them in for tea.

He remembered: a long splinter in his thumb pad. The smell of frying sausage and onions. Being told to wash his face, and never wanting to. White crockery and forks. When he cleared the table afterwards, taking one thing at a time. A plate to the sink, then going back for the spoon, a third trip for the glass, a fourth for his knife, because after the table was cleared, then it was homework time.

Hollis drew maps. He invented entire continents on paper. Mountain ranges and seas, small towns (pop. 32,000); stretching, empty wastelands. Everything had detail. His towns had roads, back streets, alleys and lanes, and things apart from the usual sort. Instead of a fire station and post office, Hollis' towns had things like a flap in the street that lifted up for you to scramble into and hide beneath, and a snail racing track, and a town cannon. He told his mother they were for a Geography project, and she said: "I see."

Sitting with her pencil in Gordon's notebook, Ma would say things like: "If $3 + x2 = y+2$, then determine the value of x."

And to Hollis: "What are those wobbly lines for?"

Topographic lines. Used for drawing mountains. Jagged and concentric rings that tightened and tightened as you came to the summit. "You write the distance above sea level in the gap between each ring," he said. "And then whoever's looking at the map knows that *this* ring," and he pointed at the highest, inner point, "is 91,530 feet about sea level, and *this* ring," showing her the furthest out, "is just a foothill." Then he looked down at Gordon's notebook, and saw that she had sketched, without him even realising it, the most beautiful and detailed picture of a dog.

"You are such a clever boy," she said. Ma was all spiral chestnut hair, and the smell of coconuts. When she stood, she seemed to be about sixteen feet tall. "Drawing all those maps." She swept Hollis up, and her flowing sleeves flapped around him like a too-small duvet.

Dad soon came home. Hung his trench on the hook, leaving it sagging there like an empty man; took both his train tickets out of his wallet, held them together, frowned at them as though the time and date confused him, and came in, said: "Hello, dear." He kissed his wife with dry lips, and threw the tickets into the kitchen bin, as he always did.

His father was a good four inches shorter than Ma. It seemed incredible that they lived together at all.

He leaned over to look at Hollis' map. Hollis had drawn a house face on, which you weren't supposed to do. In the middle of making the map, he'd started this dwelling from the wrong perspective, and before he knew it, he'd drawn a double-fronted gable house, with a curving roof like the one on the Chinese takeaway in town. It was all wrong, he knew that, but not how to put it right.

Dad frowned slightly, peering down at the paper. "Son," he began.

"Hollis," Ma said. "Why don't you put your homework away, and go into the living room to watch TV with your brother?" She was smiling and had her hand down Dad's back.

He must have caught Ma somehow. Probably in the same way that he and Gordon had once trapped a vole – by luring it in with a morsel of peanut butter, then pulling away the twig with a piece of string and catching it under the box.

The house phone had a long, shimmering ring, which peeled throughout all the rooms. He remembered a time it rang once around Christmas: tinsel on the bannister in a glittery cobweb, a Wednesday, when Gordon was at football practise. Dad had his usual conversation on the phone: "Yes. I see. Of course. I see. Well, I'll come down right away. Thank you. Bye-bye." And standing in the open living room doorway with Ma in his arms, rubbing her back and saying things like: "I'm sure it's nothing. Just stay here, Helen. Let me go and take care of it." The hallway light glowed out into the driving rain, throwing golden light upon every drop. It had seemed for a moment as if his father were the taller of the two.

It shouldn't have happened. That was what Dad said later on – a freak accident. The wind had been blowing much harder than usual, and the rain throwing itself down like it did. Gordon had been crouching by the wall, trying to screw his boots in properly, when the car came around; the road was slippery with the wind and the rain, and Gordon had been standing in a place where the coach had told him not to stand; all these things meant Gordon's death, a memorial service in a cold, stone church, and his burial in a cold, scrubby churchyard.

They were all a little quieter that Christmas. Dad spoke as though he wasn't sure of his voice, and Ma overcooked – a turkey the size of a battleship. It was lovely, rich and golden, and none of them felt much like eating it. Later, Hollis saw her go out of the back door, and dump it where the neighbourhood cats would find it, still almost whole.

She and Dad both became kinder. Dad would put his hand on Hollis' head, and leave it there, as if he had forgotten it. He said: "We need to get used to being a family now – just the three of us." Ma hugged him and held on a little too long.

Gordon's old things were in a corner of the garden. The trowel used to dig the trench, his stick-gun. It seemed wrong to leave them out there, and wrong to bring them into the house. He didn't know what to do or who to ask, and in the end brought them in on a day when Ma wasn't looking.

He brought them upstairs and put them in the box with Gordon's Lego. It felt illegal to touch the bricks, even though Gordon was no longer there to say: "Don't touch my stuff, squirt."

Gordon's plastic bricks he was touching, raking through with his hands. It was Gordon's bricks that he was using to build a house, a town hall, a police station, a school, a hospital, a rocket station, a canoe carvery. He didn't mean to, but there he was, doing it, and before he knew it he was sitting there with a whole city spreading out there on the base board before him, with a Lego man in one hand and a four dot roof tile in the other, and Ma standing in the doorway watching, and smiling.

But before he could say anything to her – apologise for being in Gordon's room, for touching Gordon's things – for not leaving it exactly as it was, with Gordon's toys and books just where Gordon had left them, she had already gone, leaving Hollis sitting on the rug with the base board and the bricks. She had not said, "Come on, Hollis, time for your homework."

He remembered staying where he was and finishing it all off. A roof on the church, windows in the houses, a man in a car going down the road. Flowers on greens. He thought he should take it down to show Ma, she who had always liked his maps so much. This was just like a map, but in three dimensions. That was what he was going to explain to her.

Dad's key rattled in the lock, and Ma went down the hallway to meet him, a thing she'd started doing now.

Hollis stood up, collected the model carefully, and walked over the landing to the bannister.

Ma and Dad were standing in the hallway below, Dad still in his jacket and hat, his briefcase on the floor beside his feet. She was resting against him, her back rising and falling.

He stood, holding the model town over the stairs. Watching his parents hold each other on the welcome mat: the sight of his father's hands in his mother's hair. Those hands rubbing softly, gently, down his mother's back. And mother, leaning over so far that she seemed almost to have fallen, a tree's broad trunk making a bridge over running water.

I WANT YOU AROUND

Tiny packaged soaps, folded towels on the bed, that's my kind of scene. Comfort and service, rather than weathering the elements. You still don't know that I'm really an indoors girl.

I hid it from you at first, scared that if you knew, you might think us incompatible. If you'd known, you might not have wanted to go out with me at all. There's never been a good time to tell you the truth. I liked to see your eyes shine at the prospect of cooking all of our meals on an unstable stove, whose narrow feet couldn't exert a decent hold in the long grass, and so I would pretend to be excited too: excited about eating food that was always partly cold, and always sticky, and seasoned with flies; about it getting dark too early for us to do anything other than go to sleep; about the strange sounds outside the tent that would wake me in the night. I made out that I liked spending all of our holidays cold and wet, that any misery at tramping the hillsides in a pair of wet socks was trumped by the surrounding natural beauty. I've learned more than I ever cared to know about the outdoors, including that no hiking shoe is ever truly waterproof.

Yours is a spot on the sofa on the left-hand side, between the doorway and the window. Mine is a spot besides yours, between you and the doorway, with a slightly different view of the television. We sit there in the evenings. Like commuters on the train coming home, washed-out dishcloths of human beings who had thought that their lives would be more fun than this, we watch and sit, too tired to talk. The brightly-coloured shapes move before us on the screen, and we look at them until it is time to go to sleep again.

We were watching the news, like we always were. A reporter on an anonymous high street was asking passers-by what they thought of falling retail figures last quarter. One woman she stopped had a grey face, pale from days under artificial light. I looked at you sideways, and your skin was the same colour. A thought hit me, sending words out of my mouth before I even knew what I was saying. "Let's go camping again."

You jumped up and ran to get the maps. *Is this really what I want*, I thought, as I heard you pulling the box out. A camping trip could take us anywhere. You are mad on remote locations. Once, when we hadn't been able find a campsite quiet enough for your liking, we'd walked for miles with our rucksack straps carving valleys into our shoulders, until you'd spotted a rocky outcrop. "How about here?" you'd said. There hadn't been any ground flat enough for a good pitch, and I'd woken in the middle of the night, crushed against the edge of the tent with your elbows wedged into me on one side, and a barrage of tent pegs lodged in the other. You'd slept like a log the whole night.

"We could go to the North York Moors." You flattened out the map. Tracing bridleways lovingly with your right index finger, you glanced at me sideways, a whisker of mischief in your grin.

"Wherever you like," I said. *It would only be for a couple of nights*, I told myself.

The weather reports all disagreed with one another, and I had no idea what to pack. I watched you put your own bag together silently on your side of the bed. You always seemed to know instinctively what to bring. I never did and didn't want to ask. In the end, I brought a handbag umbrella, shorts, a pac-a-mac, sunblock, and a fleece.

When it came, the weekend was hot, and we caught the Dales Bus from the station. Its windows were wedged closed, the air stifling. Heat rested closely on my face, clamping itself to my cheeks and forehead. All the way up and down the hills, a Daddy Long Legs, his wings fluttering on the glass, banged his mandibles on the windows, trying to get out.

"Look at the Scar," you said, when we came up to Malham. The light shone upon the rock, the crystals in its arching belly glittering at the sun like a thousand stars. The top of it rose high into the blue, and beneath it, dozens of coloured squares and triangles of canvas, tiny as postage stamps, crowded in the green beneath. "We're not camping there," you said. "Look at those idiots." Between the tents, a border collie barked in excitement at a young child throwing a frisbee. I watched sadly as the campsite disappeared from view. They had a shower block there.

With the OS map folded open, you looked up at some indefinable point, and rang the bell to get off. The bus drove away, leaving us on an empty single-track road by a dry-stone wall, without a house in sight. Miles of green stretched away in every direction. "This way," you said, climbing over a stile.

I followed you. Tall nettles and docks grew up around the tightrope-narrow path, leaning their heads towards one another at chest height. "There's a farm down here where we can pitch the tent," you said. "Come on, slowcoach." There was nothing to do but do as you said. I didn't know the way.

The green obscured everything. Leaves and stalks crossed, and all I could see through the cellulose web was your back, your brown t-shirt as you walked away. "This is the life, eh?"

The heat hung across my face like a wet cloth. "Beautiful," I said.

"It's almost a shame to pitch the tent." You vaulted a stile into the next field. "With the weather like this, we could sleep in the open air."

I put my boots on the wooden steps, over the wall. Something sharp in my rucksack drilled into my spine. The ground on the other side was covered in cow-pats. Black flies, their blue wings glittering, ran over them with spindly legs. I stepped over them, carefully, onto the clear grass beyond. "The weather report said it might rain overnight," I said.

Hands on hips, you rolled your shoulders back and lifted your face to the sun. "Hmm," you said. I looked around. Two small stone buildings, which looked like bunk-houses or sheep shelters, with gaps in the walls for windows and doors, were on the top of the hill. They were so far away they looked tiny. Down in the valley, wriggling dry stone walls marked out fields of different shapes.

"There," you said. You pointed down the hill, and turned to me, smiling. A group of grey buildings huddled together in the distance. "That's the farm." You looked excited, like you had done often in the early days.

At last being in sight of the end, I hoisted my things up on my shoulders, and followed you down. Our shadows came long, crickets chirping in the grass as we swished our hiking boots beside them. Something in your kit clanked softly, a pan against a tin mug, beating an uneven rhythm with every other step. Faraway sheep bleated to one another across the distance. Little lambs returned high-pitched cries plaintively, their light hoofs thumping in the grass.

The last few steps we walked on concrete. The ground beneath us was badly laid and lumpen, and littered with wisps of straw and hanks from sheep shearing. A fat-faced tabby lay on the barn roof, closing its eyes lazily. In the barn, footsteps, busy with some other job, rustled through the straw. We leaned against the five-bar gate, waiting for someone to come.

The farmer appeared after a few minutes, on his way to get something else done. Though he was a young man, his face was heavily lined. Beneath a rounded pug nose, a full-lipped mouth grimaced in sunken cheeks in a face that habitually wore a frown. "What do you want?" he asked.

I suppose he gave us permission to camp. At any rate, he pointed us in the direction of a fallow field behind the barn as he walked away. You called after him, "Can we light a fire?" and he gave a grunt that could have meant anything. You hauled your bag happily onto your shoulders, climbed over the gate. "He won't mind," you said. I knew then that you were going to start one anyway.

The groundsheet rattled as I unravelled it, and you started to gather stones for the fire pit. I looked around for a flat pitch, the spot where it would be least uncomfortable to sleep. The grass had been nibbled flat by sheep, and their round droppings lay everywhere. I straightened the sheet out on the ground, thinking wistfully about hand basins. Feeling around my bag for the tent pegs, I found instead my torch, a chunky thing with a thick rubber handle. I switched it on and off a few times in the darkness, to check that it still worked. It did, and I took it out and laid it next to the beginnings of the tent for later.

"I'm going to get some wood for the fire," you said.

"You go." I put my hand on the tent-sticks. Getting the wood never took long. It would be dark soon, then cold, and a fire would be all we had to entertain ourselves. Pulling the pegs loose, I heard you walk away in the direction of the trees.

Putting the tent up is easy. I put the sticks end to end and wriggled them through the canvas; the top over the groundsheet, pulling it tight with the tent pegs. Over that went the top, carefully kept separate from the inners to keep everything dry. By the time I'd finished, the air had grown cool. The moisture laying on my skin grew clammy and I shivered, pulling on my fleece. I unzipped the tent door and laid our sleeping mats and bags inside.

You were still gone when I came out. I looked down to the trees. If you were hunting around the undergrowth for dropped twigs and branches, you would be well hidden. Wiping the sweat from my face with a dry flannel, I perched on one of the larger fire stones to wait.

The moon grew sharper as the sky darkened, casting a weak light over the grass and walls. Shadows formed beneath the jagged edges of the stones, making shapes in the black. It was strange for you to be gone so long. I wondered where we were and pulled the map onto my knee. The torch light brightened the pictures and increment lines, and I tried to read them by its narrow circle. The bulb bleached the green lines to nothing. Symbols showing farm buildings seemed to litter every square. For the life of me, I couldn't work out where we were, and half an hour after starting to look, my torch went out.

I thought I ought to walk down a little way to see if you had fallen and couldn't get up. I didn't think it would be like you. You aren't the sort of person who hurts himself. All the same, I thought I would go, and I got up and set off towards the trees.

It was a long walk, longer than I had thought, and there was no path. My thighs hurt. I had already done enough walking for one day. As I walked, I kept glancing up at the stars, but I didn't know them. You were the one who knew the names of the constellations. You'd draw lines in the air and say things like, "There, you see the handle? That's the Big Dipper." To me, they were just clumps of light, some close to each other, some further apart.

They were thick, the woods. I saw it when I came up to them. Hundreds of trunks clumped close, shutting out the sky.

Standing between two firs, I called your name. There was no answer. I took a couple of steps in, and the dark closed over me. It felt colder under the trees. I called again. Each way I looked, I saw the same wood, mossy on all sides; no landmarks. It's no good us both being lost, I thought. Turning, I followed my own steps carefully back out. It must be the matches, I decided. The ones you brought had got wet somehow, and you had gone down to the village to get new ones. That was the sort of thing you would do. In these places, the nearest Spar can be miles away, and keeping track of time is not your strong point. Turning, I made my way back carefully.

It was too cold to sit out any longer. Inside the tent, the sleeping bags were in wrinkled lines, like worm-casts on the beach. I crawled into my all-weather breathable bag, zipped it all the way up around my ears, and snuggled down gratefully.

The tips of the grass rippled against the outer shell of the tent like thousands of tiny pairs of hands. Drifting off at home is to be sung to sleep by a lullaby of groaning pipes. I missed them. A tiny thing with little clawed feet ran across the ground. I could hear its belly scraping along the earth. Snuffling with a nose either broad or pointed, it sniffed, breathing into my right ear, pushing its way under the top sheet, crinkling up the groundsheet. It probably had parasites. I turned my head away, thinking of the rats in our old house, scratching the floorboards as they ran around at night. The next morning, dark-eyed with lack of sleep, you'd marched down to the estate agents to get us out of the tenancy contract. I don't know what you'd said, but our shamefaced landlord had come around the same day to help us pack. The brute was breathing in my ear. I drew my arm up over my chest to get away from it, and knocked my torch to the ground. It scurried away.

Under me, a living carpet of beetles and bugs went about its business, crawling over one another to get to the places insects go. At home, you would have got up and taken them away from me in a glass. A breeze lulled against the outer sheet, and I screwed my eyes tight closed. Folding my arms across my chest, I thought about you walking back from the village in your t-shirt, getting blisters, with a lighter in your pocket. I wondered how long you would be. I waited for you to come.

HARMONY GROWS

When the baby came – pink-skinned, feather-haired, heart beating so hard it pulsed all over – in her little arms, her almost see-through head, I said: "There's something wrong. I can feel it."

In the bloodstained white of the delivery room, Shaun hushed me, picked her up.

"Listen," I said. "Please."

He was glowing all over, a bowling ball polished to a high shine. "Don't be daft," he said. "She's perfect."

The hospital sent us home after seventeen hours and I could hardly believe I'd had a baby. Everything at home looked fake. The walls. Carpet. The cot in the centre of the living room.

The living room carpet was a moat a foot wide around the cot. On two sides, the three-piece suite, another the TV, and the other the kitchen doorway. I touched the sofa, the back, the arms, before taking the risk of sitting down. "Jesus," I gasped. I was still seeping down there, and the pain was a pair of scissors opening and closing. Two nights I'd been awake.

"What's up with you?" Shaun asked.

When you're that tired, you can argue over something or nothing, and to me his voice was the sound of a rusty gate swinging in the wind. I lowered myself down carefully, trying not to tear anything open. The baby was crying and her face was so puce it was practically blue. "She's not right," I said. "Look at her."

"She's only a day old. Give her a chance."

We'd said we wouldn't start. The new baby was supposed to bring us back together. So I kept my mouth shut, for the sake of keeping the peace.

In the afternoon, my parents brought Cody, my oldest, and there was laughter and shouting, and also their dog, pink helium balloons, soft toys, pink clothes, tiny shoes, and the house was full of my Mum and my Dad and a three-year-old as well as a one-day-old, and they'd all brought stuff with them and of course everybody wanted to hold the new baby.

"Put the dog out," I said, but nobody seemed to hear.

In this new world, I was a shadow crossing the ceiling. Somehow, during the course of three days – the Tuesday, when I'd been pregnant, and the Friday, when I'd had the baby – I'd gone and turned invisible. "Hello?" I said. "Hello, can anybody hear me?"

Mum and Dad's dog was a shelter dog that still had plenty of the shelter on her. The bitch was nervous around people, children, and in enclosed spaces. The house wasn't big at the best of times and at that moment, it felt tiny. We were all crammed in and the dog was barking sort of generally. I felt sure it could scramble up and bite the baby when we hadn't even given her a name yet.

"Oh Shaun, she's beautiful," said my Mum. "Look, Cody, your new baby sister, isn't she gorgeous?"

"How about something to eat?" Dad said. "It's about that time, isn't it?"

Of course they were all starving, but nobody had thought to bring any food.

"What about names?" Mum asked.

I fell asleep for five seconds and woke looking at the baby's hand. It dangled from the blanket, pale and ghostly. "Hamberly, Hamberly," Cody shouted. "Hamberly."

"What's she saying?"

"Harmony," I murmured, only just managing to stay afloat. "It's one of the names on our list."

She could never be comforted, even when I did everything you're supposed to. When I cuddled her, Harmony hardened in my arms like a Belfast sink. Her screams were the sound of nails down a blackboard inside a car being crushed. Even when she wasn't screaming, I could still hear it.

The health visitor came. She was a pinched woman in a lavender fleece. "You have to *persevere* with breastfeeding," she said, and she used a fake knitted tit and a play dolly to show me what a failure I was as a mother. "Like this," she said. "Hold her like a rugby ball." I had never played rugby. "You need to give her the best possible chance of latching on."

When I tried, Harmony turned her head away, her mouth red and scrawny, like uncooked meat. "It's useless," I said. "I don't think she likes me."

"Of course she likes you." The health visitor turned away, and started gathering her things. "You're her mother."

At night, Harmony turned violet. Fingers, lips, eyelids. I sat up with her, watching her breathe, feeling for a heartbeat. I hardly dared touch her. I hardly dared not to.

When Shaun came down in the mornings, the colour had mostly gone. She'd turned pink again, as though deliberately proving me wrong. Under her nails, though, you could still just see it.

Shaun reached into the cot and flew her up into his arms. Three hours she'd been asleep, a record. "Don't," I said. "You'll wake her."

"She's fine," he said. "You're making a big fuss over nothing."

It was the fact of growing that seemed to pain her. She cried for hours at night, and as she got bigger, so did the noise. It was even starting to wake Shaun. She'd start at midnight and sometimes go on until four, five in the morning. Those of us living in the house with her became the living dead. Shaun said he hadn't known it was possible to be that tired and still live, and before too long, he caused an accident at work. He fell asleep at the wheel of his forklift and drove it fork-first into a pallet of little cartons of UHT milk. The milk made a lake all over the warehouse floor and they had to close the whole section for an hour to clean it up. Shaun's boss gave him a verbal warning and made him take a week off work unpaid.

He came home in the middle of the day in a bad mood.

"I've been telling you and telling you there's something wrong with her," I said, "but you won't listen."

"You're the one who can't get her to sleep," he said.

Over in her playpen, Harmony lay still and flat as a matchstick, legs straight, feet pushed together, arms by her sides. There was something uncanny in the way she laid like this. She often did it. It meant she was unhappy, I think.

"Alright then, we'll take her to the doctor," Shaun said. "Maybe then you'll stop going on about it."

"I can see how you might be worried." The GP looked young, as though she should still have been in school. "But all of this sounds normal. Some babies cry more than others, that's all. Why don't you wait a little while? These things usually clear up on their own." She offered Shaun a prescription for sleeping tablets and waited for us to go away.

Unluckily for her, I'd been onto the NHS Choices website. "We're not leaving until you refer us to a specialist. I want her seen at the rare genetic disorders clinic."

Harmony started. Cooing at first, the starting signal for something else. Something much larger. The GP glanced at her, smiling and cooing. *You won't be doing that for long*, I thought. Sure enough, Harmony stiffened. Going red in the face, bracing her legs stiffly against her pushchair. And within minutes, she was shrieking loud enough to be heard in all of the upstairs consulting rooms.

Any other time I would have tried to stop her. Not that day. I wanted the doctor to see what our lives were like.

"They won't see you." I lip-read from the doctor.

I picked Harmony up, to do a show that I was doing all I could. Like usual, she curdled hard as sour milk, and the screaming got louder. "This is what she does," I explained, showing the doctor Harmony's angry, purple little face. It was like trying to hold a conversation by a live construction site. "Sometimes for hours at a time."

I waited a minute. Watched the GP's hands twitch, as though she was trying to stop herself from putting her fingers in her ears.

"About that team at the hospital," I said.

The doctor looked at the baby and then again at me, at us, sitting in cushioned chairs in her consulting room, refusing to move.

"Alright," she said. "Alright."

By the time the clinic letter came twelve weeks later, Shaun had left. It said to go with somebody, but I was going alone, and this time, nobody was going to tell me I was imagining things.

Harmony was growing into a strange toddler. She had a broad face, limpid eyes, and when I put things into her chair to go and catch the bus – blanket, cushion, a soft toy to make her more comfortable – it was hard to know whether she knew they were there. On the bus, a woman peered in at her, expecting to smile, then rearranged her face out of a shocked expression. She turned away and pretended not to see me. Other people looked at her once and then looked away.

In Dr Suleiman's office, I saw how wrong she looked, her face out of proportion, her legs and arms all stiff, and she was laying there almost at forty-five degrees. "Now then," he said, "I understand we're having trouble sleeping, is that right?" His voice sounded like the shipping forecast turned all the way down.

"That's the least of it," I said. "She hates being touched. She lays there all stiff. Sometimes she goes blue, absolutely blue, at night, so blue that sometimes I think she's – you know."

Dr Suleiman came out from behind the desk, all five foot six of him, NHS lanyard, stethoscope. "It could be any number of things," he said. "Let's have a look at you, shall we?"

Harmony liked Dr Suleiman. A strange thing, I'd never seen her like anybody before. He put on a pair of funny glasses that he had hooked on his shirt pocket, put the stethoscope to her heart, and she giggled. "Well then, how does she eat? Solids, baby food, are ok, and her poos, are they normal?" Dr Suleiman was only the second person I'd ever seen Harmony smile at.

"She likes you," I said.

He listened to her heart. "And you say she's got no words – no words at all?" He got up and went back to his desk. "Just to be on the safe side, let's get you an MRI and a couple of genetic tests. Try not to worry too much," he said. "We'll soon find out what's going on."

We had to wait a good while for the MRI as well, Harmony and Cody and me. Although I wasn't sure how well she could hear or see, I still gave her things to play with. I moved her playpen out of the front room and brought in a bean bag. I'd lay her on it so she could watch YouTube videos with her sister. She had tough legs, but she wasn't using them. The most movement she did was to stiffen them, then go floppy again. She could turn her head from side to side. That was about it. When I played with her, I jingled a set of bells on a stick, and she'd turn her head to look at them. Sometimes she'd smile.

Shaun hardly ever came to see us. He came once, and looked at Harmony with distaste, as though she was something disgusting on a plate. "What have you done to her?" he asked. "She used to be normal." He said, "That MRI's probably going to show that she's brain dead, anyway."

"Get out," I said.

"Fine." Off he went, practically whistling.

The morning of the MRI scan, I set my alarm for five a.m. to be sure we all got to where we needed to be on time. We were supposed to be at the hospital for eight thirty, but before I could even get up early, I was woken by the sound of thumping on the girls' bedroom floor.

I was up and out of bed before I was even awake. Darkness in the house lay across everything. "Girls," I whispered. "Girls, are you ok?"

Harmony was laying on the bedroom floor, face down, hand thumping against the carpet. She'd fallen out of bed, it seemed. Luckily she slept on the bottom bunk, so she'd only fallen a few inches.

I lifted her up, and she was trying to make a sound. Babbling with a flapping, disobedient mouth. At least she wasn't crying. She seemed happy enough.

"Harmony's not tired," Cody said. "She says she wants to get up."

"It's too early," I said. "Both of you go back to sleep." I put Harmony back in the bottom bunk and tucked her in tight as a sausage roll, to stop her from rolling out again. "I don't want any more silliness tonight." I would need to get some kind of gate or side wall for the bottom bunk, I saw, but where could you buy such a thing?

I went out of the room, closing the door quietly. My phone said it was three forty-eight, which made it hardly worth going back to bed, so I got up and got dressed, or at least I meant to. It later turned out that I fell asleep on the sofa fully clothed, with my coffee going cold on the kitchen side.

There were all sorts of nurses on the ward, each in a different blue. Nurses, healthcare assistants, physiotherapists, occupational therapists. Tabards or polo shirts. The one who came to collect us was in dark blue. Smiling and capable. She put a Peppa Pig transfer onto Harmony's arm, and slid a canula in it. In a moment, Harmony's eyes fluttered shut, and the nurse was able to put the radioactive-proof mask over her face.

"That anaesthetic won't last ten minutes," I said. "Just you wait and see."

"Rough night?" She stopped in the middle of going. Her trainers, a pair of bright orange Nike running shoes, squeaked on the lino.

"This morning she got me up at four," I said.

"Here, look," she said, as she was turning to go, "Why don't I make you a coffee? You look like you could do with it."

I looked at the bright new face of my daughter, which in sleep seemed to have been sloughed clean. There was a translucence to her skin. It was fine as a spiders' web, and in her cheeks I could see a thin network of blooming green veins, interconnected, like branches on a tree. "Thank you," I said, and the nurse's hand on my arm touched me like a kiss.

Six weeks later, a letter came inviting me into Dr Suleiman's office for a chat.

Harmony was getting big, and she no longer fitted into the stroller. Her torso was too long, and her arms were too thick. But she wouldn't go out of the front door unless she was in it: she'd create a fuss loud enough to wake the dead, so I'd worked out a way to get her inside.

By removing some of the cushioning and loosening a few bolts and screws, I could widen the seating area and put an IKEA bag where the old chair had been. It formed a sort of hanging cushion into which Harmony could easily fit. She liked it. When she was in it, she'd pull the blue fabric crinkling around her face and legs, closing her in as though she was inside a chrysalis. It didn't look very comfortable, but when I tried to put blankets and so on with her, she didn't like that either.

So I put her into her IKEA bag chair, wheeled her out of the front door and onto the bus, where we got some very odd looks, and took her to Dr Suleiman's office. "Good morning," he said. "Just you today?"

"She's in there," I said. My Mum had taken Cody to nursery.

"Right," he said. Crisp white paper, silver ballpoint pen. "Shall we have a little look at Harmony's results?"

He switched on a light box and showed me a picture of my daughter's brain. There was one bit that was dark, another bit that was light. Dr Suleiman used the end of the silver ballpoint to point out different bits — amygdala, cortex, occipital lobe — and as he went on, did his best to explain. It seemed there was a part of Harmony's brain that was smaller than it ought to have been, and there was another part that wasn't there at all. Parts of Harmony's brain, he said, in somebody with her condition, would continue to shrink until it disappeared. "I'm afraid that your daughter has an extremely rare and incurable mitochondrial disorder," he said, "which only about eight other children in the world also have."

"Eight?" I was thinking, what the hell is mitochondria, and also: what do you call the opposite of winning the lottery?

"In Harmony's case," he said. "You have this issue in the brain here, with the cells dying and not being replaced, and she also has a genetic condition which causes hyperactivity in some of her glands. This condition can, in some children, cause elephantism of the inner organs and I'm sorry to say," he went on, "that the abnormalities in Harmony's brain are not at all connected to the genetic disorder, and we have no idea what's caused all of this to happen."

"You're telling me she's got two things wrong with her?"

"I'm afraid so."

"And you're also saying you can't tell me why it's happened."

He opened his large, soft hands. "I really wish you hadn't come alone for this. You ought to have somebody with you."

"What about Cody? Does she have it too?"

He started to draw something on his pad. It looked a bit like something you might see in a butcher's shop window. "Unlikely," he said. "You almost certainly would have noticed it by now if she did."

At last, Harmony had clocked where we were. She wriggled her way to the edge of the IKEA bag, let my phone slip out of her hand and fall onto the lino, and gazed at Dr Suleiman all googly-eyed, as though he was Liam Payne from One Direction. "Ah, look," he said. "She's saying hello."

"Cody's got a different Dad," I said. "Could that be why?"

"It's possible," he said. "Would you like to join a parents' group? There's one monthly, run by the occupational therapists."

"No." Harmony's hands, floury and pink, squirmed over one another as she watched him. On the floor beneath her, my phone continued to flash with the pink pig and the white fence, only now the screen had a big crack down one side.

It was incurable, he said. She would always be this way. Squirming hands and boat-oar legs. Behind every child her own age in everything but height. She may never talk. Would always do the same things, over and over. She'd be a twenty-one-year old watching Peppa Pig, if she lived that long. It was a life-limiting condition, Dr Suleiman said, but the advances in medical care made it hard to give an accurate prognosis. He had never seen another child with Harmony's condition and didn't know what to expect. In many respects, I knew more than he did.

He sent me on my way with a drawing of Harmony's insides, and a diagram of an ordinary brain. I'd taken a picture of her scan on my phone, and taken a note of the name of the condition so that I could look it up when I got in.

Soon after, people started coming to the house. Women with lanyards and pull-along boxes full of toys and binders of notes. A physio, a speech and language therapist, then a woman in a thin cardigan, who said she was a multi-sensory impairment worker, who I think must have got the wrong house, a nurse, another nurse, a different nurse, a music therapist, an occupational therapist, a man in a suit, who I think maybe just came to check we weren't going to sue, then another nurse, a play worker, then the physio again. The letters, my god. The kitchen workshop and cupboards and drawers were full of them.

"You really ought to start keeping these in a folder," Mum said. There was a letter from Dr Suleiman with a footprint on it, from where Cody had stamped on it whilst dancing to Ariana Grande. "Look, you've missed an appointment."

"Honestly Mum, some days," I said, "I don't know whether I'm coming or going."

"I'll get you a calendar," she said. "Or how about a big diary, one of the A4 ones with the pockets in the back?"

"Mum, no. I'll just keep it all on my phone."

"You need somewhere to keep them all," she said, and she brought me one anyway.

Our days were full and so was the house. Being at home for Harmony's appointments was a full-time job. The house was full of bits of equipment. A special soft posture chair for Harmony, better than the bean bag they said, splints with pink butterflies to correct her legs, and also a pair of big clumpy black shoes that she tried to pull off as soon as you put them on her. The music therapist had showed me shimmery silver fabrics and tough rubberized toys and instruments that didn't break easily, so I'd bought her as much stuff like that as I could afford.

The place became a graveyard of things they'd left. Splints she'd been fitted for, then outgrown. Harmony was growing so fast she had stretch marks. She was almost at school age and bigger than your average seven-year-old. When I took them both out, people thought she was older than Cody.

Her skin was turning a darker pink, apricot-hued, like the inside of the shell. Every day, she looked more and more like me. She was growing taller, and strong. She'd taken it into her head to start walking, and she was strong, and fast. She could get into any doorway and rip any toy apart in seconds. At night, she'd get up and thump around all over the bedrooms until I got up and put her back to bed.

This was hardly the girl that Dr Suleiman had warned me about, a sickly and ill girl, a girl who needed to be coddled.

Every time she came, Mum took about a hundred photos and videos. She claimed these were for Dad, but my phone had started pinging with money, notifications from my banking app, small deposits: ten here, twenty there, and I knew it wasn't coming from Shaun.

"Oh," Mum faked casual, "that'll be from Shaun's Mum. You should get in touch to say thanks."

I was full of shards of hot metal, every vein, every pulse. "I didn't ask her to send money."

One of Harmony's favourite toys was a squeaky dog toy from the Pound Shop. I'd wanted to get some of the same sort of toys that the play therapist brought, chunky things with thick handles and bright colours. They were made out of a special kind of rubbery plastic that wouldn't break no matter how hard they were thrown. The closest thing I'd found to them were these dog toys. Harmony didn't seem to mind. She didn't know the difference.

"She's as angry with him as you are."

"How would you know? How would either of you know how angry I am?"

"I'm just saying," she said. "By the way, have you read this letter from the local children's hospice?"

I didn't want to take her to the hospice, not at first. She wasn't dying. But they were offering me – or rather, Harmony – eight overnight stays a year, and more than anything else I wanted a good nights' sleep.

It was in a place tucked so far back from the road you wouldn't even notice it. The taxi took us through a small estate of new build housing, a curving line of boxy, sand-coloured houses, and through a narrow lane thick with a row of young trees either side.

When the taxi driver let us out, I looked and saw so many paper butterflies. Pink, sugar paper butterflies in upstairs windows, a large tissue paper butterfly, royal blue, sellotaped to one of the downstairs windows. These hadn't been here before, when we'd come to look around.

"She'll be out of this building in a second," I said. "She'll be out of that doorway and across the car park and into the road before they can stop her."

"They know what they're doing," Mum said.

"Mum, I don't like this." I looked through the taxi window at Harmony, suddenly small as a scrap of paper. "Let's get back in the taxi and go."

Harmony had got her shoe off. She'd undone it and kicked it loose, into the footwell of the taxi. She stared right at me, triumphant as a cup winner, and pulled her sock off. Mum hadn't noticed. She was around the boot of the car with the driver and all of Harmony's bags. "Have we got everything?" she said. "Splints – medication – the letters from the doctor?"

Harmony travelled with more luggage than I did. She needed twice as many sets of clothes as anybody else, letters and prescriptions, tubs of protein thickener for her food, sun cream, a hat, and a second hat, in case she lost the first hat.

"Hello." A woman appeared in a green top, with a pen sticking out of her hair. "You must be Harmony, and Harmony's Mum. I'm Andrea." I don't know how she did it, but she'd got past me and to my daughter and in under a minute, she'd unclipped her, taken her out of the car seat and picked her up. "Off we go," she said. "Shall we take you inside and get you sorted?"

"Wait a minute," I said, "her shoes."

Already Harmony seemed to have forgotten I existed. She clung to the woman and pointed to something in the building's doorway.

"Come on, love." Mum shut the boot, counted money out for the driver. "Look how happy she is." She was weighed down with everything, two bags on her right shoulder, another on her left. All I was carrying was one sock and one shoe. "Let's go and get her settled in, and then we'll go."

At the door, Harmony reached for a giant paper Tigger, smiling, her loose little foot kicking against the woman's side as though she was playing a drum kit. Her foot had been out in the open air for almost a minute now. I could see the edges of her big toenail starting to go a very pale blue.

"Let me put her sock on."

Harmony barely even noticed. She wasn't even looking at me. She'd spotted another little girl inside and was pointing and babbling excitedly, a pre-verbal auctioneer trying to sell something at a high price. For all she cared, we might have already left five minutes ago.

"You will look after her," I said, "won't you?"

"Of course." Andrea smiled. "You don't have to leave her yet, if you don't want to. You could come in and have a cup of tea?"

Mum pretended not to look at her watch, eager to get home for the dog, and I looked at my daughter, smiling as she'd never smiled before, kicking against the poor nurse as though she was peddling a static bike.

"No," I said. "I think it'll be ok."

DEAD LETTERS

We lived in the mailroom, moles with blunt nails and teeth. They taught almost every subject at the University and my supervisor, George, claimed to have learned most of it. Campus I rode through on the mailroom bike, delivering whichever of the mail had the right address, which was far from all of it. It was a big place. History, Physics, Mechanical Engineering, Music, Sculpture, Mathematics, Student Welfare, Counselling, Modern Languages, Classics. I won't go on. Medicine. The campus was too large and the buildings too complicated. Some of the departments you could only enter through a back door. In my first six months, I'd got lost quite regularly. After two years, I still did, so there was no hope for the mail.

Administrators and academics sent all sorts. Letters, phone chargers, geology samples. Scraps of embroidery. Video and audio tapes in obsolete formats. Once, an internal memo with 'I love you' scrawled on the back. We weren't supposed to open things, but sometimes there was no reason not to. So much of it was so wrongly addressed, it never would have found its way home.

Professor Alan Mack's birthday card had come back to us for the eighth time, returning with a new scar, bleeding glitter all over my fingers. Seven people had written across its front: *Not Known In This Department.*

My supervisor George was a human rabbit of a man. Big ears, whiskers. "That card needs to go in the bin," he said. In July, the place emptied out, and there wasn't much to do, apart from sorting out the shelves. We could sit on the lawns, pretend we were there legitimately, enjoying the sun and getting paid for it. George let me come in late and leave early.

There wasn't enough to do to make coming in for a full day worthwhile.

"Why?" I said. For me, finding Professor Mack had become a game. Somebody who didn't have his home address was trying to wish him all the best. Somebody from a conference, maybe. The academics went on these jaunts. Some were hosted at our place. Every January, there was a jousting festival. A guy came with a jerkin and some buzzards, which he fed meat on the Union steps.

It was no use looking on the website. The staff pages were hardly ever updated. "I'll find him eventually," I said. "You watch."

The shelves, the Lost Shelves, looked like something out of a documentary about hoarders. Letters and envelopes shoved together like the cards of a flower press. Unopened parcels from M&S and Toast, things the staff had had sent to work, but which had been misaddressed and had ended up down here. There was a load of books from book suppliers and academic publishers, for which George had a terrific nose.

"Here's one for you." He took one out of its cardboard sarcophagus, handed it to me. "This is right up your street, isn't it?"

The book was titled *Feminist footnotes: re-reading correspondence from England's forgotten women letter writers, 1724-1792*. It was hot, post-exam celebrations over and done with, campus deserted. Rabbits colonised the quad lawns, twitching wide-eyed and whiskered in places where undergraduates normally gathered. George and I had opened the big doors to the sorting room, but it was still dark, deep as a sunset, dust motes swirling. "You might as well have it. There's probably a copy in the University library anyway."

Funny, I'd always thought I'd come back to university, and here I was. During term time, I rode around campus on the mailroom bike, wondering how everybody, even the first years, seemed to know where they were going. My time at university hadn't been like that. I'd arrived lost and stayed that way. Knowing where to sign up, where to go for this lecture, that seminar, how to sign up for modules, which day and time to go to library induction, working out how many credits you needed, which bits of the course were compulsory, all the different dates for signing paperwork for student loans, bank accounts, uploading coursework to the e-portal, there was so much of it, and I couldn't keep track. They'd put me in a houseshare with eight strangers, in a room at the top of the house with a puddle-shaped stain on the ceiling which dripped onto the bed. Nobody else had wanted this room, which was why it was less expensive than the others, but still pretty bloody expensive.

There seemed to be an extra person living in the house, somebody nobody had invited, a person who crept the stairways and halls at night and opened doors with a creak, peeking in through the gaps. I could never tell whether I was in the house alone, and hated being there, but I didn't know my housemates well enough to knock on their bedroom doors for help. At Christmas, I'd left, leaving most of my stuff behind, and had never gone back.

I delivered letters and other things there now. The administrators, blank-faced, dark-cardiganed, in the department where I'd once studied, took the mail from me without even looking at my face. Even if they had, I doubt they'd remember me. I'd not even made it to the end of term.

Professor Alan Mack's card returned a tenth, eleventh, twelfth, thirteenth time. Half the card was showing out of the envelope. It had been through Earth Sciences, English Lit,

French, Geography, History, and Law. They were running out of space to write *Not Known In This Department* on the front. "Dora," George said, "For God's sake."

He was about to go on holiday with his wife and their two children. Every year the same villa in Greece, which had a pool with sun loungers, and a good restaurant a short walk away. It was ten minutes to the beach, not that they ever went. "It might be the only birthday card he gets," I said.

"Don't spend too much time on it, OK?" A nod to performance management. "And remember, you don't need to come in every day next week."

I swept stuff from the Lost Shelves into the mailroom trailer, cycled it across campus to the big bins. When term started, we would need the space.

With George away, I was getting stuff done much more quickly. I didn't bin any of the books. George had already taken any that interested him, travel guides and maps mainly, but even he wasn't interested in the academic works.

In the university library, there was just me, the librarian, a handful of international students. I walked right in in my mailroom uniform and stayed.

The stacks were showered with light coming down through the glass-domed ceiling. With the undergrads gone, it was quiet. Nobody was loudly reliving last night's night out or shoving their phone in somebody's face to play them their best ever Spotify playlist. A postgrad whispered her way through the shelves, dedicated, frowning, and I started reshelving books.

These wouldn't be Dewey categorized. They would be Dora categorized. I was no librarian. I put the books where I thought they ought to go. It seemed better, more right somehow, than chucking them into the Biffa bin behind the campus theatre.

In the morning, I shelved twenty books and in the afternoon, sat in a pool of light near a recessed doorway that led to a fire exit, reading a book of letters written by a woman who had been dead over two hundred years, and was now as good as forgotten.

On the way to catch the bus home, I bundled up Professor Alan Mack's card with the sole letter that had arrived that week for somebody in Maths and posted it through their letterbox. The door was all locked up: everybody here was on holiday, too.

Should you want a place to charge a phone from ten years ago, the mailroom was the place to go. We kept plastic stacker boxes of ancient technology. We had chargers for phones they didn't make any more. Sometimes people came looking for things: "I'm stuck without my glasses," they'd say, or: "I think I left it plugged in in the postgraduate common room." Had somebody from my first-year house tried to return my stuff, they might have brought it to a place like this. "We don't know where Dora's gone," they might say. "Let's try sending her things to History." But I wasn't there, not anymore, so everything – the textbooks I'd pointlessly bought from the reading list, a Bluetooth speaker I'd acquired from somewhere, my Yellow Card for drinking in the pub – would have ended up on a shelf, until somebody said: "Just bin it. It's obvious she doesn't go here anymore."

Out of everything I'd left, the only item whose loss I truly mourned was the £40 textbook which I'd bought brand new, only used twice and which, I'd since discovered by delivering mail to the campus bookshop, I could have sold second-hand for £30. First week of lectures: unloading this tome from my bag whilst the girl sitting beside me watched, staring as

I took out everything – pens, pencils, notebook; I'd been too embarrassed to bring out the Bronze Age laptop, which had been through two pairs of hands before it had arrived in mine, a beast that took fifteen minutes to start, flashing like a funfair with malware pop-ups I couldn't delete – as though I was some creature she'd discovered in the corner of a damp room, and she'd said: "You know you don't actually have to *buy* everything on the reading list, right?"

Opthamology, Physics, Psychology. It was September, the students were coming back, and Professor Alan Mack's card was disintegrating.

"Colour me impressed," George said. He took up his place behind the Customer Services desk. George liked to work there. It gave him a sense of importance, and first dibs on the Amazon parcels. "You've got the whole place clear. If it wouldn't put me out of a job, I'd recommend you for a promotion. Are you still on about that bloody card?" he went on, fingers twitching. "At least open it to find the sender's address, so you can return it."

Fat chance, I thought. George never returned a thing. "You only want to see if there's money in it."

"Any money that was in there is long gone. You're like a dog with a bloody bone with that thing," he said.

I borrowed an internal phone directory and started ringing around, asking everybody if they knew Professor Mack. Theatre Studies, School of Cultural Studies, Zoology. I wore my fingers to nubs. Somebody suggested I try Human Resources. "They'll know," they said.

The lecture theatres were large and if you sneaked in at the back, nobody saw you. I had learned a lot this way. Carbon-dating. Molecular coding. Serial composition. Romantic poetry. For all I knew, Professor Mack might have created some of the knowledge I was siphoning off. This place was full of academics who were the first person to think of something, and who had then written one or more books about it, made a whole career out of their ideas. We never saw most of them. The really clever ones spent afternoons hiding in their offices, snoozing maybe, heads laying in a shaft of light. Their names were on the front of the prospectus but, catlike, they were clever at avoiding people. If they didn't want you to see them, you never would.

I caught half an hour of musculo-skeletal anatomy, then went back to our cubbyholes under the university. "You've been busy," George said. "Somebody called for you from HR. I asked, has she been doing something she shouldn't?" He looked tense, sweating. "You know I've always thought very highly of you, Dora. You're conscientious. Get the job done. We're a good team, aren't we?" Boiling water from the kettle into two mugs. "That's not to say you couldn't go onto better things. I know you'll be leaving me one day. When I took you on, I said to Adrian, I don't think she'll stay six months, this one. She's too smart." He handed me a mug. "I'm surprised you've stayed this long, to be honest."

The lady from HR looked as out of place as a Pomeranian at a dog fight. Swinging her shoes over the dusty floor, she told me Alan Mack had worked in English Lit, that he'd been an expert in folk tales and legends, specialising in the late 16th century. He knew more than anybody else how peasants of the day had spoken, what they believed, how they celebrated their rituals. He was a specialist in it. "So what happened to him? Did he retire?"

"I had to do a bit of digging even to find out his specialism," she said. "It was before my time." She glanced over at the goat skull which George had found, liked the look of, and placed on the Customer Services desk. "Is trying to get a card to him a good use of your work hours?"

There was a not-so-hidden disciplinary warning in that question. "I'm out delivering the mail anyway," I said. "It's not as if I'm going out of my way."

"You phoned every department in the internal phone book," she said. "You phoned me."

She held her hand out for the card, and I told her I didn't have it. It had been delivered to Music that day, I said.

Later, I went back to the library. Without a login, I'd been unable to access the electronic catalogue, but now that I knew what shelves to look on, I looked for his books. There were two: collected fairy stories, and a book of myths. The stories were over four hundred years old. I didn't know how he'd gone about collecting them. I took it off the shelf, slid the card between its pages, and put it back.

Back in the mailroom, George was busy tossing envelopes into sorting slots. He was wearing a frilly, palm print dress pulled on over the top of his uniform. "Would this fit you?" he asked. "I don't know whether it suits me."

"It doesn't. And take it off. It isn't yours."

"Alright." He pulled off the dress, and the specs he was wearing, and threw them into a box that we kept for such things. The box would fill with hearing aids, contact lenses still in their boxes, sometimes even crutches. "Where've you been, anyway?"

"Library." I joined him beside the pigeonholes. Left to right the holes went: Engineering, Psychology, Theatre, Student Welfare. These fitted the order I did the rounds in. There was a system to it.

"Again?" he said. "Anybody would think you were hankering after being a student again. Don't you think it's about time you went back?"

"Maybe I like it down here," I said.

"I don't think you do."

He was right, even though I was pretending to him and to myself that he wasn't. Of course I didn't like it in the mailroom. Who would?

One year after, I broke ground. Upwards onto solid ground, blinking, the sun splintering into my eyes, rainwater on broken glass.

All of the other students were younger than me by four years, apart from the few who hadn't taken a gap year, who were five years younger. I was twenty-three and felt about a hundred. The house I lived in was shared with three postgraduates, who eyed me with suspicion, who ate noodles with their feet tucked up on the living room sofa, no doubt wondering when I was going to reveal my true undergraduate partying nature. "I'm your age," I reassured them. "You don't need to worry." The age thing wasn't completely true. Two of them were actually younger than me.

In the lecture theatres, the seminar rooms, with the notebooks and pens and a slightly newer laptop, the knowledge I acquired was legitimately bought and paid for. At the end of term, I would write papers. I would prove what I had learned. I was eager. I was ready.

In those first lectures, the other undergraduates chattered like sparrows. They had the kind of unassailable confidence you can't learn in a one-day, self-help workshop. They'd had it when they were babies. It was written in their genes.

Up there, the air was light. Breezes blew, sent papers flying off the desk. You never knew when something would come along and surprise you. Every day was different. Knowledge was given out in lectures and hidden in the pages of books in the library. Whether or not you went to the lectures was considered optional by most of the students. I went to everything, and I made sure I never lost a thing. After classes, I scrabbled around on the floor, checking for notebooks, my charger, the types of things that the others all too readily left behind; I made sure that anything I'd taken out of my bag went back into it again, because I didn't want to end up back down there. Under the rest of the University, scrabbling amongst the shelves, looking for lost things in baskets and on the shelves. I had started living above ground, a woman with sun on her face.

ACKNOWLEDGEMENTS

Firstly, I want to thank the writer-friends and creative friends who have been there either at the start of the journey, or at various points along the way. Thank you to: Jenna Isherwood, Mason Henry Summers, Max Dunbar, Faith Radford-Lloyd, Claire Bayabu, Sam Francis, everybody at Fictions of Every Kind, and to Robb Barnham, Bryn, Mike Bird, and Vinnie, the Fictions of Every Kind house band. Particular thanks to Rachael and Alice Rix-Moore for the knitting-based art pranks, and for knowing that the best kind of creativity is always at least 60% illegal. Many of these stories were published in lit mags or online, or were written as part of a project, and it was these little bits of encouragement that made me keep going when it all felt a bit thankless. Huge thanks to Stephen Moran at Willesden Herald, Barney Walsh at Litro online, Ra Page and all at Comma Press, Becca Parkinson, Tania Hershman, Fiona Gell at Leeds Big Bookend, Linzi Tate Smith who supported the Northern Short Story Festival in its early days; Darran Anderson of the Honest Ulsterman, Peter Spafford and Rosie Shackleton at Chapel FM / Dortmund 50; Gianna Jacobson at December magazine, and Nathan Connolly and Wes Brown of Valley Lines Press.

I particularly want to thank writer-friends Glen James Brown, Naomi Booth, Stu Hennigan and Barney Walsh, for being there at various points along the way. Short story writing is a solitary business at the best of times, especially for somebody who taught themselves by listening to podcasts and reading books in the library, and who didn't know any writers at all when they started out. Thank you, all of you, for making it slightly less grim.

A special thank you to Krishan Coupland and EC Shephard, for organising the best writing residency of all time at Alton Towers, and for making it so fun and so weird (in a good way) that I still think and talk about it, years later. Thanks also to poet Suzannah Evans for the two-person Facetime-based writing retreat in lockdown that led to me writing 'Coming Attractions.' Thank you, Andy Hill and to Ali Johnson at First Story, for your brilliant work in placing writers in residence, including me, in Academy schools in Leeds and Bradford. I also want to thank Anthony Clavane for his recent support and advice.

Finally, the biggest thanks of all to my parents; my friends Hannah, Carrie and Ash, and to Ricky, without whom none of this would have been possible.

Many of the stories in this book were previously published elsewhere: *Backstreet Nursery* was first published in Short Fiction 8;

Dance Class was first published in Willesden Herald 7;

Weak Heart was first published in the Honest Ulsterman and later in Verse Matters;

The Stonechat in the Alton Towers Liminal Resident publication;

Meet Yourself Coming Back was in the Dortmund 50 publication;

Toro was first published on the Dead Ink website;

The Life of Your Dreams was first published in the LS13 anthology;

The Gordon Trask was first published in Disclaimer magazine;

Maps of Imaginary Towns appeared in Litro Online;

Top Dog was first published in Toasted Cheese online lit mag;

Genus was first published in December magazine;

An earlier version of *I Want You Around* appeared in Cutaway Magazine.

About the Author

SJ Bradley is a writer from Wakefield. Her short fiction has appeared in various journals and anthologies including *Conradology* and *Resist! Stories of Uprising from Comma Press, New Willesden Short Stories 7, Queen Mobs, Litro magazine,* and *Untitled Books.* Her first novel, *Brick Mother*, and her second novel, *Guest*, are both published by Dead Ink. She is the editor of the Saboteur Award-winning anthology *Remembering Oluwale*, which is available from Valley Press. Her work as an arts organiser involves the non-profit literary social Fictions of Every Kind (which ran for 10 years), The Northern Short Story Festival and the Walter Swan Short Story Prize. She is also a teacher of creative writing including short story writing courses for Comma Press and First Story in Leeds and Bradford. She's on X at

@bradleybooks.

About Fly on the Wall Press

A publisher with a conscience.
Political, Sustainable, Ethical.
Publishing politically-engaged, international fiction, poetry and cross-genre anthologies on pressing issues. Founded in 2018 by founding editor, Isabelle Kenyon.

Some other publications:

The Sound of the Earth Singing to Herself by Ricky Ray

We Saw It All Happen by Julian Bishop

The Unpicking by Donna Moore

Imperfect Beginnings by Viv Fogel

These Mothers of Gods by Rachel Bower

Sin Is Due To Open In A Room Above Kitty's by Morag Anderson

The Dark Within Them by Isabelle Kenyon

Secrets of the Dictator's Wife by Katrina Dybzynska

The Process of Poetry Edited by Rosanna McGlone

Snapshots of the Apocalypse by Katy Wimhurst

Demos Rising Edited by Isabelle Kenyon

Exposition Ladies by Helen Bowie

The Truth Has Arms and Legs by Alice Fowler

The House with Two Letterboxes by Janet H Swinney

Climacteric by Jo Bratten

The State of Us by Charlie Hill

The Sleepless by Liam Bell

Social Media:

@fly_press (Twitter) @flyonthewallpress (Instagram and Tiktok)

@flyonthewallpress (Facebook)

www.flyonthewallpress.co.uk